Saturday Night Date

Maud Johnson

SCHOLASTIC BOOK SERVICES
New York Toronto London Auckland Sydney Tokyo

Cover Photo by Owen Brown

ISBN 0-590-31963-9

12 11 10 9 8 7 6 5 4 3 2   2 3 4 5 6 7/8

Saturday Night Date

A Wildfire Book

WILDFIRE TITLES
FROM SCHOLASTIC

chapter
1

Sometimes when I think about Charlie Peterson and remember everything that happened between us, I marvel at my mind not breaking when my heart did. If Charlie had died, I'd have grieved although maybe I would have been able to accept it better, because death would have been out of my hands, an event I couldn't control.

But Charlie didn't die. He just stopped wanting *me*. I died inside, yet I kept on breathing and going to school and doing my chores at home. After a time I even managed to smile and hide the aching hurt which had become as much a part of me as my eyes or my hair or my arms and legs.

Everything began the Saturday after Thanksgiving — a raw, sleety November day. At least, that's when it began for me. I realized later that Charlie had made his decision earlier without mentioning it.

Helen, my older sister who was a sophomore in

college, was at home for the holiday weekend and she came upstairs about twenty minutes to seven that Saturday night, poking her head in the bathroom. I'd showered and shampooed my hair and was getting ready to blow it dry.

"Wendy, Charlie's here," she said.

"This early?" I plugged the blower cord into the electrical socket over the sink. "What possessed him to come before seven when he told me he'd pick me up at eight? Tell him to read a magazine or watch TV, and I'll be down as soon as I finish my hair and get dressed."

"It's something about the party you're going to. He said the party has been called off."

"Why?" I gave her a puzzled glance.

"Charlie didn't say but he seems awfully solemn and — "

She was interrupted by the brass knocker on the front door, which banged with a heavy metallic *thwack!* Both of us jumped as the loud sound echoed through the house.

"That must be Stan for me. Strong hands, huh?" she added, smiling. "Listen, Wendy," — quickly she was serious again — "Mom and Dad have already gone out, and Stan made our dinner reservations for seven o'clock, so he and I won't linger here. You'd better put something on and find out what's bothering Charlie. He looks as if he's just lost his last friend."

She disappeared, pulling the bathroom door almost shut without completely closing it. Charlie Peterson was in and out of our house so much he felt enough at home to answer the knock at the door. I could

2

hear voices, Charlie's familiar one and the deeper tone that belonged to Helen's date, Stan Maynard.

She'd recently met Stan, who attended a state university near her college, and it was obvious he liked her a lot because this was the fourth date they'd had since she had come home Wednesday. He lived in Oakwood, Virginia, just as we did, but he and Helen hadn't been in the same high school and didn't know one another until recently. It was Stan who'd driven her home from college Wednesday, and he had offered to take her back to her school Sunday afternoon. The way she glowed when she said his name let me know she considered him to be more than a casual boyfriend.

I wrapped a blue bath towel around my hair like a turban, put on my underwear, and zipped my white quilted housecoat to my chin. Helen's comment about Charlie aroused my curiosity, and it wouldn't matter to him if I wasn't dressed. *He has seen me looking worse,* I thought, and laughed at my reflection in the mirror.

Charlie and I lived on the same block and we'd known each other as far back as either of us could remember, which included prekindergarten days. Now, we were high school juniors, both of us seventeen, and friendship wasn't a deep enough word to describe the love we shared.

That Saturday night I purposely waited on the second floor until Helen and her date left, not wanting Stan to see me in a housecoat. Our stairs were straight at the top and curved a little at the bottom as they came down into the living room. My fuzzy slippers were so soft they muffled any noise on the steps, and I was three or four feet behind Charlie before he realized I was there. He was by the fireplace with his back toward me, not doing anything, just standing in one spot with his jacket collar turned up around his neck, as though he was outside in the wind instead of in a warm place.

"Hello," I said and caught my breath. Helen was right. I'd never seen him so solemn. "Charlie?" The one word was a question and my voice broke at the strange, frowning expression on his face.

"The party's been canceled," he announced. "Wes phoned me a little while ago. Angie's grandfather died suddenly in Chicago late this afternoon, and her whole family is flying there tonight."

The party was to have been at Angie MacLawhorn's house, and since she and Wesley Andrews were going steady, it was understandable for Wes to call everybody. What didn't make sense was Charlie's reaction. I was sure he didn't know Angie's grandfather personally, but he appeared as glum as though it was his own grandfather who'd died. Angie's party wouldn't have been a big deal, just six or seven couples, all of us school friends, sitting in the MacLawhorn basement recreation room drinking Coke and eating potato chips and cheese. Angie's father was a salesman for a cheese processing firm, and the MacLawhorns always had plenty of cheese in their refrigerator.

"It's too bad about Angie's grandfather," I said. Charlie mumbled, "Yeah," and continued to stand in that one spot as if his shoes were glued to the rug. He seemed tense, his upper teeth pressing into his lower lip.

Moving nearer to him, I reached out my hand for

his. He stepped backwards, and I recoiled as if he'd slapped me. He'd never backed away from me before.

"Charlie, what's wrong?" I asked.

"Nothing's wrong." He stared past my shoulder instead of into my face. "Your folks aren't home, are they?"

"They're at the hospital visiting Mom's boss who had surgery last week."

"Are Helen and that Maynard fellow coming back here any time soon?"

The conversation was weird. Charlie didn't sound like himself. Usually he was relaxed and smiling, only at that moment he appeared to be tied in knots.

"Stan is taking her to dinner," I said. "I guess they'll be gone at least a couple of hours."

Watching Charlie as he stood in my living room that November night and seeing the strange, smoky look in his eyes, I felt uneasy and wasn't sure why.

"What difference does it make if we're by ourselves or if my family is home?" I asked.

"I want to talk to you, Wendy. Privately."

"Okay, talk. What's the big mystery?" The words died on my tongue. All of a sudden I was scared and didn't know what I was afraid of. "Charlie . . ." My voice quivered as I said his name.

He glanced at me and looked away, his cheeks bright red for a moment with the crimson color going as speedily as it had come. I waited, not knowing what to do. Charlie was so ill at ease I felt panicky, and after twenty or thirty seconds that seemed like an hour, I said, "What is it you want us to talk about?"

Part of me was troubled at the way he was acting, and the other part was becoming a little annoyed. I wasn't really angry — I loved Charlie too much to be angry with him unless there was a very good reason — but I didn't enjoy being kept in the dark.

"Wendy, I . . . I've been trying to . . . to have this talk with you for a couple of weeks."

After jerking that one sentence out, he hushed. I opened my mouth to tell him he wasn't making sense, but he cut in before I could speak.

"Don't stop me, Wendy! Let me finish because if I don't do it in a hurry, I won't be able to say what I have to say!" He drew a huge, gulping breath. "It's not that I don't think you're a wonderful girl, because you are. The greatest. I've always known it, and I like being with you and kissing you, but . . . but we ought to date other people. Both of us. You've never gone with any guy but me and I haven't — Oh, good gosh, Wendy! Don't look at me that way!"

I didn't know what "that way" meant or how I was looking at him. The room was spinning. All the familiar furnishings, the sofa where Charlie and I had sat so many times and kissed, the wing chair with the squashy green velvet cushions, the desk and the lamps and the bookcase by the fireplace, all of it was whirling in front of me until I was dizzy. I could not believe what I'd just heard. *Date other people?* Charlie and me? No way. *No way.*

"Aren't you going to speak?" he asked hoarsely.

It took all my strength to make my vocal cords respond. "Is this your idea of a joke?" I said. I felt like I was yelling, although the question came out as a whisper.

"Do you think I'd joke about anything this serious, Wendy?"

"You mean you don't want us to date? To go steady anymore? Why? I don't understand — "

"Next year we'll be seniors, and the year after that we'll both be in college." His voice was growing stronger. "I think we ought to have more experience. And the only way to get it is to branch out. To play the field."

My knees felt as flimsy as cotton. The desk chair was nearby and I sat down on it because I was trembling. For a second I was hot, the pulse in my temples beating hard, and the next moment I was frozen.

"Wendy, are you okay?" he asked. "You look funny."

I wasn't okay. I didn't know if I would ever be all right again, but I ignored his question because I had one of my own. It was a terrible question, and I steeled myself to ask him.

"Are . . . Are you trying to say you've stopped loving me?"

"I guess I'll always love you, Wendy. As a friend. We've been pals for — well, I can't remember when we didn't know each other. But . . . but now, it's different. Different from what it was — from the way it's been since we began going steady two years ago. I guess what I'm trying to get across is that I don't think I'm in love with you anymore. That's the only term I know to — don't stare at me like I've just shot you or hit you! It isn't anything you've said or done. Honest. It's simply that my life is nothing but a routine. A grind. I go to school and go to work at the drugstore, and the rest of the time I'm with you or I'm eating or sleeping — and that's it. All of it. Just plain nothing but an awful rut."

When I didn't reply because I couldn't, he groaned. "Can't you understand?" he pleaded. "Don't you want some excitement in your life, too? I feel like I'll split wide open if I keep on like this. No action. Nothing to break the monotony. You're bound to feel the same way, if you'll only think about it."

No, I don't. I don't, Charlie. Being with you is all the excitement I need. I could never stop loving you and wanting you, not even if I tried.

The words burned my mouth, but I didn't utter them. Instead, I asked another question, and then a lot of questions.

"When did you stop loving me, Charlie?"

"I just told you. I still care about you. You're like my family and I want us to be friends. Always. Pals. Only . . . only we ought to be free to date other people."

"But when did you decide you didn't want to date *me*?"

"It's not a snap decision. I've been thinking about it for a while."

"For how long?"

"I can't give you the hour and minute, Wendy."

"Who is the — " I swallowed hard, trying to steady myself. "Who is the girl you're going to date?"

"No special girl. I don't have anybody picked out and already lined up, if that's what you mean."

If he thought I believed that, he had to be crazy.

Maybe he hadn't asked some other girl for a date, but he had to know which one he wanted. Was it Angie MacLawhorn — if she and Wes called it quits? Charlie had always thought Angie had lots of personality. Suzanne Howard? "Sexy Suzanne" was her nickname at school. Behind her back, of course. Did Charlie want to date Karen with her breathtaking beauty and her warm smile?

I tried to focus my eyes on Charlie, but his face was a blur.

"Is it sex?" I burst out. "Are you trying to tell me that I'm just not sexy enough to please you?"

"No! I've just explained — "

Before he finished the sentence, I was sobbing. I didn't want to break down, but the tears wouldn't stay back and my face seemed to be cracking. Breathing was hard, and it was impossible for me to think clearly with so much pain jabbing at my heart.

"Wendy, don't cry! Please don't!" He stooped down in front of my chair but he didn't touch me. At any other time, when Charlie knew I was troubled, he'd have held my hands or put his arms around my shoulders; when he didn't do either, I knew he meant all those terrible things he'd just said, that he truly wanted us to break up.

"I . . . I'm sorry," I mumbled. "I . . . I don't mean to cry, but I can't help it."

He reached into the back pocket of his jeans and handed me his handkerchief. I blew my nose and wiped my eyes, but the tears continued to roll down my cheeks.

"Wendy, I wouldn't hurt you for the world. You know that. But this is something I've been thinking about and I had to tell you how I feel. I didn't want to go behind your back and date another girl. There hasn't been a good moment to talk about it — until tonight." He stood up and sighed. "I guess I haven't been very tactful."

I didn't answer because I couldn't. The hard sobs were trapped inside of me, stifling whatever I might have said.

"Dragging this out won't do either of us any good." He sighed again. "I'd better go. You'll be okay by yourself until your parents get here, won't you? They should be home soon, because visiting hours at the hospital are over early."

He was inching toward the front door. *Charlie, don't leave . . . please . . . please . . .* The silent words were a prayer.

Through the mist of tears in my eyes I saw him open the door and close it carefully without looking back. His footsteps clattered across our narrow porch and grew fainter as he reached the sidewalk.

chapter
2

When Mom and Dad came home half an hour later I was still in the living room, huddled on the sofa with my feet tucked under the quilted housecoat, the damp towel still on my hair. The tears had stopped but they began again when I saw my mother.

She hurried to me, not even pausing to take off her coat. "Wendy, what is it?" she asked. "Are you sick? Why aren't you at Angie's?" She put her palm on my forehead, then slid her hand to the back of my neck the way she always did if she thought I had fever.

I told her and Dad what happened, repeating everything Charlie said, my voice quivering with the words coming out in hesitant phrases instead of complete sentences. Her eyebrows lifted in disbelief, and Dad cleared his throat several times.

"Charlie isn't in love with me anymore," I moaned.

"I doubt that, Wendy," Mom answered. "I'll bet he comes back in the morning, apologizing and trying to make amends for upsetting you."

"But he told me he just wants us to be friends. Pals — that's the term he used. He came right out and said it and — oh, Mom — " I buried my face in her shoulder, pushing my cheek into the tweed of her coat. I was crying again, so hurt I didn't care if I lived or died.

"Wendy, dear, don't" she said in a soothing voice as she moved her hands up and down my back. "If you keep on like this, you're going to have a headache, and tears won't solve anything. Charlie must have been worried about something. About his job or schoolwork. Everything will be fine tomorrow. You'll see. You and Charlie have such a special kind of relationship that — "

Dad cleared his throat again, louder that time. Raising my face from Mom's shoulder, I saw the two of them exchange glances with Dad shaking his head. He was trying to communicate something to her.

Brushing my fingers across her shoulders, I said, "I've cried on your coat."

"No harm done. It'll dry. It was already damp from the weather. I hope Helen won't be out late because it's such a horrible night, and there are icy spots on the road. Wendy, go wash your face with cold water. How about a nice cup of hot tea or cocoa? That should make you feel better."

I might have smiled if I hadn't been so miserable. Helen and I often joked in private about the fact that no matter what crisis happened in our family,

Mom believed something hot to drink would ease the situation. Occasionally it worked, but this time tea or cocoa wouldn't help.

My mother insisted on making tea, and I dutifully sat across from her at the kitchen table and tried to get the scalding liquid down. Dad was in the den, the variety of voices and music coming from that direction making it apparent he was switching from one television channel to another. Mom chattered on and on, going into endless detail about the hospital visit; how cold the weather was; did I still want the navy and white checked coat I'd admired earlier in the fall in The Teen Shop, because it might be reduced for the after-Thanksgiving sale if it was still in the store. I knew she was attempting to get my mind off Charlie, as if that were possible.

Curls of steam rose from the cup, making my chin warm and moist. I stared at the golden amber tea with the slice of yellow lemon floating on top and forced myself to take small sips, but finishing it was a futile effort.

"I guess I'll start homework," I said, clutching at any excuse to be by myself. Concentrating on textbooks at that particular moment was a joke.

"Wendy, don't go upstairs and begin crying again. You can study tomorrow. For now, come in the den and watch TV with your daddy and me."

I shook my head. She didn't insist, and I was grateful to her for that. *I won't cry,* I told myself. *I won't . . . I won't . . . if I can hold back tears . . .*

At the kitchen door I forced myself to look at Mom. "Thanks for the tea," I told her.

She smiled, and I suppose she thought I felt better and that Sunday morning would bring peace and happiness to Charlie and me.

Almost everything in my room reminded me of Charlie. Not the furniture, but almost everything else. The two stuffed rabbits on the bed had been a gift from him one Christmas. He said he couldn't decide which I'd like better, the pink or the blue one, so he bought both.

He had made the lacquered wooden jewelry box on my chest of drawers in industrial arts class. On my desk was a pencil holder made from a juice can, his camp crafts project the summer he was ten. He'd covered the can with brown plastic material which resembled leather and stenciled "Wendy" on it, the letters in an uneven, slanting circle around the middle with the W and Y almost touching, since too much space separated the E, N, and the D.

Years afterward when we were fifteen and were in my room one Sunday afternoon cramming for a history test, Charlie picked up the juice can and rolled it between his palms, offering to get me a "real pencil holder."

I wouldn't hear of it. "The day you came back from camp and handed me that can—and it wasn't even my birthday or Christmas — I was on cloud nine," I told him. "It meant you liked me and up to that time, I hadn't been sure. You were forever telling me I must be part horse since I had a ponytail. But to have you make something for me, with my name on it, no less, was proof you'd been thinking about me."

"Gee, only ten years old and I was already in love," he teased and grinned. We laughed about it, and I suspected that, secretly, he was glad I liked hanging on to the childish things he'd given me, especially those he made himself.

Pictures of Charlie were everywhere in my room. His last yearbook picture was in a frame on the chest of drawers, and snapshots had been stuck under the rim of the mirror. On the desk there was an enlarged photograph of the two of us taken at one of Angie's parties: Charlie and me sitting very close together on the couch in the MacLawhorns' basement, his arm around my waist.

More pictures were in a box in the closet, along with things I had kept over the years. Valentines. Corsage ribbons. Programs from school events. A blue crepe paper streamer which was part of the gym decorations for a dance.

Maybe saving those things would seem silly to some people, but not to me. The mementoes marked special moments, times when Charlie and I were happy, secure in the knowledge of how we felt about each other.

Now, he wanted us to stop being close. To stop dating. He just wanted me to be his pal.

Pal. I shuddered at the impersonal word. Suddenly, I got up and stared at my reflection in the mirror over the chest of drawers, halfway expecting to find an ogre looking back, but except for tear marks on my cheeks and red rims around my eyes, I was the same girl I'd always been. On the outside. I had the same light brown hair and blue eyes. Most of the time my complexion was clear, and my hair was clean and shining. My figure was okay, but not perfect. I wasn't beautiful and couldn't fool myself by pretending I was, but I wasn't hideous, either.

Pretty might be the word to describe me. Charlie had often told me he thought I was pretty.

Turning away from the mirror that terrible November night, I reached for the two stuffed rabbits and held them to my face. They were as soft and cuddlesome as ever, while I seemed to have become a chunk of cement.

I'd always considered Charlie my best friend as well as the boy I loved most in the world; I didn't want any-boy but him holding my hands or putting his arms around me or kissing me. Not ever! I didn't want anything to be different between us. Charlie might be able to turn his heart off and on the way he would a Bunsen burner in chemistry lab, but my heart didn't operate like that.

chapter

3

Helen woke me Sunday morning. I felt a hand on my arm and heard somebody call my name. My eyelids were so heavy it was a struggle to open them. Helen, wearing jeans and a thick white ski sweater, was standing by the bed. The room was a mass of pale gray shadows that made me think it must be early, not much past daybreak, a ridiculous hour for my sister to be rousing me.

She turned on the bedside lamp and the grayness changed to a muted yellow glow. Suddenly, everything about Saturday night came surging back into my mind. Charlie. The terrible conversation he and I had. My mother's effort to comfort me. Sobbing in the night as I held the stuffed rabbits.

"What time is it?" I asked Helen.

"Twenty minutes after eleven."

"Eleven in the morning?" I sat up, glancing toward the gray sky visible through the window. I couldn't believe I'd slept that late.

"Right. The radio is forecasting more sleet, and possibly snow for this afternoon, so Stan is taking me back to school early. That will let him get to his college by nighttime. Mom's making brunch, and she says for you to come on down. I told her you were still asleep, but she said for me to wake you — that if you sleep all day, you won't sleep tonight."

"I'll get up, but I'm not hungry." My voice trembled. I didn't want to smell food, much less try to eat.

"Wendy, Mom told me about Charlie. About what he said to you last night. He — "

"Has he phoned this morning?" I cut in. "Is he here now?"

She shook her head.

Tears came into my eyes. I blinked but they wouldn't go away.

"Listen, Wendy," she went on. "I know you're hurt. But maybe it's for the best. If Charlie isn't the loyal kind, isn't it better for you to find out now?"

"He *is* loyal!" I said fiercely. "Don't you dare talk about him!"

"You're actually defending him! That's for the well-known birds! I'll bet when you start going out with other fellows, you'll wind up with some guy you'll like a whole lot more than you do Charlie Peterson. He's been underfoot so long you're used to having him around, and you don't know how fantastic another boy can be."

"It's easy for you to say that," I muttered. "You have Stan. You'd feel differently if he stopped wanting you."

18

She took a deep breath. The room was very still. I wished she'd go away and leave me alone.

"I'll tell you something I've never told another soul if you'll keep it to yourself," she said. "Promise?"

My curiosity made me forget about myself for a brief moment. Helen and I were able to trust each other. I nodded and she sat down beside me on the bed.

"I do know what it is to be rejected, Wendy. There's this guy in two of my classes and during the first part of the semester he was the only thing I thought about. He's the macho type. Great body and gorgeous looks. He didn't have a steady girl, not one I could find out about, but he didn't ask me for a date until the middle of October. That's all we had — one date. Maybe I wasn't in love with him, but it sure seemed like love to me."

Her cheeks were unusually rosy and she picked up a corner of the bedsheet, pleating it between her fingers. "He didn't phone and I turned down dates with other guys, just waiting and hoping to hear from him. In class he'd say, 'Hello,' and that was all. I waited two more weeks and couldn't stand it, so . . . I asked him for a date."

She breathed deeply once more. "It took all my courage. I did it after English class," she said. "I fibbed and told him I had two free movie tickets and wouldn't he like to come with me.

"But he turned me down. He said he was busy and that he'd be in touch, but he hasn't been, and seeing him on campus since then has been a nightmare. I still like him, but I've accepted the fact that there's no possibility he and I will get together."

I didn't reply because her situation wasn't the same as mine. She barely knew this fellow, while Charlie and I had been in love for a long, long time.

"What I'm trying to get across to you, Wendy," she said, "is that I didn't die from being rejected, even if I thought I would, and you won't either. I really believe it happens to most girls at some point. Happens to guys, too, I guess. After I met Stan, I was glad nothing had developed between — "

Mom called from downstairs to say the food was on the table. Helen hopped up and tugged at her sweater. Perhaps she was glad for the interruption before she made any further confessions.

"Come on down and try to drink some coffee and juice even if you don't want to eat, Wendy." She gave me a long look. "I know you feel rotten, but staying up here by yourself isn't the solution."

A glance in the bathroom mirror while I was brushing my teeth told me how awful I looked. My eyes were swollen and my skin was as blotchy as if I'd had a rash. The rough night showed in my face as plainly as if I was wearing a sign proclaiming it.

Late the night before I was sitting on my bed in the dark holding the stuffed rabbits, when Stan's car stopped outside. I heard him and Helen laughing softly as they walked to the house. Somehow, that made me all the more desolate. A little later, my parents' footsteps let me know they were coming to bed and I laid down and pulled the blankets to my chin, pretending to be asleep when Mom eased the door of my room open to peep in.

It was more than three hours before I finally slept. I ached for sleep because it would have made me stop thinking, stop longing for Charlie, but I couldn't lose consciousness. I tried, but even with my eyes closed, my brain was wide awake. Whirling.

I tried to will myself not to think about Charlie but was unable to think about anybody or anything else. A few times, I put on the bedside lamp to look at my watch, quickly turning the light off so Mom wouldn't realize I was awake. Once I went to the window, shivering without a robe and in my bare feet. The rain made a steady, drumming noise. A car came around the corner, its headlights reflecting on the shiny, wet pavement and accentuating the stark black of the leafless tree branches bordering the sidewalk. In a matter of seconds the car disappeared and the silence seemed louder than the rain.

The final time I checked my watch was at ten minutes to four. I'd never been up that late in my entire life. Immediately afterwards, I must have slept because I didn't remember anything until Helen woke me.

Our kitchen was a long room with a round table at one end where we ate most of our meals. The family was waiting for me when I came downstairs. Mom had gone to a lot of trouble to make everything look tempting, using the blue mats and the blue and white china breakfast set usually saved for special occasions.

It seemed to me my mother talked a great deal as if she couldn't tolerate silence, and when she paused, Dad or Helen would chime in. After a short time I became aware of what was happening. The family was attempting to get my thoughts away from Charlie.

The three of them ate the creamed turkey on toast

and fresh fruit salad with my mother's special dressing, while I slid food around on my plate. Mom watched me out of the corners of her eyes and finally said, "Wendy, would you rather have a scrambled egg?"

"No, thanks. This is fine. I just got up and I'm not hungry yet."

I forced a small taste but was spared having to eat more when Stan arrived, hitting the knocker just as heavily as he'd done the previous evening. In a muttering undertone Dad commented that he hoped the door wouldn't be torn off the hinges, and he added, "Helen, tell that boy to ease up."

Helen was on her feet, starting for the door to let Stan in. I hugged her and ran to my room, thinking vaguely this was the second time in a matter of hours I'd avoided saying hello to Stan Maynard — I looked far worse that morning than I had Saturday night.

It's strange what little control I had over my mind that Sunday. I put on jeans and a long-sleeved shirt, settled down at the desk in my bedroom to begin Monday's homework assignments, yet the entire time I was remembering incidents involving Charlie and me.

He and I had always known one another, our houses just a block apart. Some memories went back to childhood and others were more recent. There were a million little incidents tucked away in my mind like bright pebbles in a glass jar. The time Charlie had chicken pox and I couldn't visit him, but had to talk to him through the window so I wouldn't catch it — and I got it anyway. The afternoon when we were eight or nine and I fell out of the apple tree in old Mrs. Cummings's yard across the street — after Mom had given me orders not to go there since Mrs. Cummings didn't like children. Charlie had helped me up and taken me to his house, putting thirteen adhesive bandage strips on the scratches on my knees — he probably would have put on more except that there were only thirteen in his family's medicine chest. Both of us wondered why my Dad laughed and wanted to know who won the fight. The time Charlie came to the house to take me to a school party and I had my first long dress. He had blurted out in front of Helen and my parents "Gosh, Wendy, you're beautiful! I never noticed before."

The one memory that kept coming back was very special. It was of the night Charlie and I realized we were in love. It had happened two years earlier during the last week of May on a soft, balmy evening when it killed us to have to stay inside and study for exams.

For a couple of hours that night, we sat at the kitchen table in my house with our textbooks and class notes spread out before us, and shortly after nine o'clock Charlie announced that he didn't think his brain could absorb any more history facts.

"Mine can't, either," I agreed. "Let's stop."

I made lemonade and we carried our glasses to the backyard, sitting on the bottom step without talking much at first. A luminous glow filled the blue black sky and the moon hung just above the horizon, huge and golden. Everything smelled fragrant . . . the early summer flowers, the new leaves on the trees, the faint wind that stirred the air. I slipped my feet out of my sneakers and wiggled my toes in the cool, dewy grass.

The next day was Charlie's birthday, and I said, "I hope you'll like what I'm giving you for your birthday." I'd gotten him a record album he had wanted and a keychain flashlight with his initials on it.

"I will. I always do." Charlie leaned back with his long legs stretched out and his hands locked behind his head. "Know something, Wendy? In twenty-four more hours I'll be old enough to date."

That was an odd remark. I'd thought we were already dating, considering all the times we'd walked to and from high school together, all the evenings we sat side by side, and all the conversations we'd had about every subject under the sun. To me, those times were dates, but now, I wasn't sure what Charlie called them.

"Well, what about it?" he asked.

"What about what?"

"Are you going to date me or aren't you?"

My throat muscles were pulled tight. I opened my mouth and couldn't make a sound.

"Wendy? Are you going to sit there like a zombie and ignore what I just said to you?"

"Are . . . are you asking me for a date?"

"Is that such a wild idea?"

"But I thought . . . I mean, you and I . . ."

The right words wouldn't come. I turned my head toward him. The moon was higher, shining on his face, making his light brown hair more tawny than it actually was. He gazed at me with an expression I'd never seen before. I couldn't describe it, not then or afterwards, but I knew I would never forget it. Behind the mistiness in his eyes there was a loving look, a pleading.

"I'm serious, Wendy," he whispered. "When I find a decent job for the summer and for after school I'll have money to take you places. I don't think I could ever like a girl any more than I do you, and I'll never, never stop wanting to be with you."

His eyes moved to my mouth and he reached out almost timidly to slide his forefinger across my lips. Charlie had hugged me and he'd held my hands endless times, but that night was the first time he'd really kissed me. His mouth touched mine, feather-soft at first, and somehow his arms were around me and mine went around him and we were holding each other tightly and his mouth tasted sweeter than warm honey.

But Charlie did stop wanting me, in spite of what he'd said that May evening in the moonlight. Sitting at the desk in my room on that dreary November Sunday two and a half years later, I knew he must have found another girl, someone he cared for more than he did for me.

If he hadn't, how could he have told me he thought we should date other people? *How could he?*

chapter
4

At breakfast the Monday after Thanksgiving I told Mom I didn't think I would go to school.

She gave me a quizzical glance as she reached across the table to put her hand on my forehead. "You aren't feverish," she said. "Unless you're actually sick, I don't believe you should miss classes."

The morning routine at our house seldom varied on weekdays. Dad read the newspaper while he ate, starting with the front page and promptly turning to the sports section before he headed downtown to his insurance office. My mother worked from eight-thirty until one o'clock weekdays at a handicrafts shop. She liked to leave the kitchen neat, so I did the dishes after breakfast while she was putting on makeup. Charlie usually arrived about the time I finished, and if the weather was bad, Mom dropped us off at school on her way to the shop. On fair mornings he and I walked, as it was only six blocks.

At least, that's how it had been in the past. I knew

in my heart Charlie wouldn't put in an appearance at my house that Monday although I was still hoping for a miracle. He hadn't phoned or come near me all day Sunday.

"Wendy, if you're thinking about staying home today because you're afraid you'll bump into Charlie at school, forget it." Dad looked at me over the top of the newspaper. "You'll have to see him eventually, and the sooner you do it, the easier it will be for both of you. I don't imagine this is any more pleasant for him than it is for you."

I wanted to scream at my father, to remind Dad that breaking up was Charlie's idea, not mine. It couldn't be as hard on Charlie because it was what *he* wanted. He hadn't cared about my feelings or about how much he hurt me.

"Your father is right, Wendy." Mom nodded her head toward Dad.

I fixed my eyes on the toaster sitting on the counter by the sink because I had to look at something. A few crumbs were scattered over the shiny chrome surface. Crumbs always flew in every direction when the toast popped up.

"I don't think I can face Charlie or . . . or any friends," I managed in a shaky voice, still staring at the toaster to avoid looking at my parents.

Or endure seeing Charlie with another girl, I added silently.

"Just hold your head high and keep your tears to yourself, dear," Mom said in a sympathetic way. "If you don't want gossip to start, be casual. People may ask you what happened, and all you need answer is that you and Charlie have decided not to go steady. For you to stay home today would only put off the ordeal until tomorrow, and that wouldn't solve anything."

"You don't understand!" I burst out.

I saw them look at each other. Dad folded the newspaper and laid it on the table beside his coffee cup.

"Right now you probably can't think beyond the present," he said. "This is rough for you, Wendy. Your mother and I are aware of that. But after a while you're going to see that Charlie acted wisely."

"Wisely?" The word burned my throat. "Hurting another person is 'wise'?" My voice was a mixture of pain and sarcasm.

"I've been concerned for some time about you kids seeing so much of each other that you weren't trying to make new friends," he went on. "You ought to be dating a variety of boys while you're in your teens, instead of tying yourself down to just one; the same goes for Charlie where girls are concerned. To my way of thinking, the boy showed his maturity by recognizing the fact."

So Dad believed Charlie was "wise" and "mature" and it didn't matter for me to have one big ache. I caught my breath. If I'd answered my father, I might have begun to sob.

"It's very cold and raw this morning, even though the rain has stopped." Mom's voice cut into my bitter thoughts. "Hurry with the dishes and I'll give you a ride to school on my way to work."

But I don't want to go . . .

I didn't say it aloud. If I hadn't been so upset I'd probably have wondered if Mom was merely being kind, or if she didn't trust me to go to school after she and Dad left the house. She should have known I wouldn't deliberately disobey them.

Arguing with my parents was a waste of time when they agreed on a particular subject. I learned that before I was out of kindergarten, and they'd never permitted Helen or me to miss classes unless we truly were sick. Going to school that Monday might be torture for me, but I knew I would have to do it.

I saw Charlie first thing.

Roosevelt High was located close to the street with all the parking areas and athletic fields in the rear, and when Mom stopped I had less than fifty feet to go from the car to the school entrance. She drove off and I'd walked barely a third of the way when Charlie and Wes Andrews came around the corner of the building, walking very fast.

The boys spotted me just as I saw them, and the sight of Charlie made my knees wobble. His face turned red and, instantly, changed to an ashy gray color. I wanted to run to him and fit my hand into his, to lean my forehead against his shoulder, and to feel his arms go around me while he said it was all a mistake, that he hadn't meant any of those hurting remarks he'd made Saturday night.

I didn't do it, of course.

Wes was coming toward me and his "Hi, Wendy" was firm and loud. Charlie stopped walking — standing perfectly still as though he was uncertain — only he didn't actually look at me, just in my general direction. I realized I, too, had stopped walking. There was a half-second for me to decide what to do. Charlie seemed almost as ill at ease as I felt, and I knew him well enough to sense that he wished he was somewhere else. Anywhere else.

Perhaps he was embarrassed. I wasn't sure. At that moment he could have apologized — if he had any intention of apologizing for hurting me — and he didn't do it. During that strange half-second I knew instinctively he meant every word he'd spoken Saturday night.

Remembering Mom's advice, I kept my head as high as I could. But the effort to smile was a waste because my lips stretched into what had to be a weird grimace and my "Hello" came out in a trembling tone which didn't sound like my voice at all. I began to move toward the school door, surprised at being able to move my feet; Charlie mumbled something, which sounded a little like my name and also like he was strangling.

The boys didn't follow me into the building. I knew it without turning to see. Going down the long corridor to my locker, my heartbeats boomed like thunder. *I won't cry . . . I won't . . . I won't,* I repeated to myself, and all the time I was blinking to hold back tears.

Charlie and I were in different homerooms, but I saw him in our first period history class and braced myself for physics lab which followed. I was thankful that, for once, Mr. Willets, the teacher, insisted on assigning lab partners instead of allowing us to select our own. Neither Charlie nor I glanced at the other. I doubted if it was noticeable as there was lots of commotion when classes changed, or maybe I merely hoped it wasn't noticeable.

For me, the worst part of that Monday was lunch

hour. Charlie and I always ate together, usually taking seats at a table with other couples who were going steady. For a little while that noon I toyed with the idea of not going to the cafeteria, but the weather was too cold to spend lunch period out of doors, and at Roosevelt High the library and auditorium were closed during the two lunch hours.

While I was standing in line, my eyes anxiously searched the cafeteria until I found Charlie with Wes and several boys at a table in the back. If Angie had returned from her grandfather's funeral, Wes would have been with her, and he must have been curious as to why Charlie wasn't with me. A prickly sensation swept over my body. Had Charlie told Wes what happened Saturday night? I was positive he had. Wesley Andrews wasn't dumb. He would have realized something was amiss between Charlie and me after the scene on the school grounds that morning.

Karen Baker threw the first personal questions at me.

"Wendy — over here!" Karen gestured to the vacant place beside her as I paused at the end of the cafeteria line to decide where to sit. It was doubtful if I could choke down the soup and milk I'd bought, but an empty tray would have been conspicuous. She scarcely let me reach her table before saying, "What gives with you and Charlie, Wendy?"

Karen and I had known each other our entire lives and I liked her, but it was general knowledge that she was inclined to gossip. I needed desperately to talk to somebody, to confide in a friend, but not Karen — unless I wanted my personal problems spread all over school.

The heavy thudding in my head made my skull seem on the verge of splitting wide open, and I didn't reply to her at once. She turned sideways in her chair to look at me, and I had to say something.

"I don't know what you mean." I was very busy opening the milk carton, glad to keep my hands occupied.

"Oh, come on, Wendy! You know darn well what I mean!" She lowered her voice to a whisper. "Why aren't you and Charlie together like always?"

There haven't been many times in my life — since I was five or six years old — when I've wanted to hit another person, but that noon it would have been easy for me to slap Karen. I knotted my hands in my lap to hold them still. My teeth were clenched, and I almost lied to satisfy her for the moment. I wanted to say I knew I'd be delayed and had told Charlie in advance not to wait for me. For a wild moment I was tempted to tell her to shut up, that what Charlie and I did was none of her business, but before I could do it, Mom's words rang in my ears: *If you don't want gossip to start, be casual.*

There was no possibility of being casual although I prayed my voice wouldn't break. "Charlie and I have decided not to go steady," I said, trying to keep my voice steady. "It's no big deal."

"You what?" she gasped. "I don't believe it! What on earth happened? Was this your idea or his? Did you two have a brawl? You and Charlie — why, you're like night and day or peanut butter and jelly or cheese and crackers! You know what I mean, Wendy. You two belong together. Nobody thinks of one of you without the other."

I couldn't think of one of us without the other,

either, although I didn't admit that to her. Karen continued to stare at me, and I forced myself to taste the soup which was hot and left the surface of my tongue rough.

"Did Mrs. Marlowe give your math class a pop quiz this morning?" I asked. "If she did, she'll give my class one this afternoon. She does it every time."

"Don't change the subject, Wendy. No, we didn't have a math quiz."

She continued to stare, her brown eyes open very wide. After a full minute she said accusingly, as if I'd committed a sin, "You didn't answer my questions about you and Charlie."

"There isn't anything to say, Karen."

"Don't hand me that, Wendy."

My throat muscles tightened. "I've already told you it isn't a big deal." I measured each word out to sound convincing. "There's no need to make a federal case out of it. Charlie and I aren't concerned."

How I managed to utter such a mammoth lie, I'll never know.

Her face flushed and she began taking the plastic wrap off her sandwich. I knew by the way she hunched her shoulders forward and the jerky movements of her fingers that she was annoyed. Karen, for all her nice qualities, had never been able to control her curiosity.

Pretending not to notice, I told myself she'd accepted my explanation. Yet, I knew she had stopped her questions only because she realized I didn't intend to talk about what went on between Charlie and me.

Luckily, the conversation was cut short as Patti

Simms, a rather reserved girl, came to the table. After saying hello, she asked me a question.

"Wendy, don't you live on Hawthorne Street?" she asked.

"Yes," I nodded. "At 1402 Hawthorne."

"My family is moving to 2921 Hawthorne. That's a few blocks from you, isn't it? We hoped to wait until after Christmas, but the apartment where we've been living has already been leased and the new people want to get in as soon as possible, so we'll move this weekend."

I murmured something polite to Patti, my mind still on Karen's questions. Charlie, Wes, and Gary Lincoln, who had quarterbacked the school's football team, left their seats and moved toward the door. Charlie walked very erectly as if he was marching in a parade, his shoulders squared, and his eyes not glacing to either side.

Karen and Patti got into a discussion about a book which was assigned reading for one of their courses, and I was relieved for the breather to try to get my thoughts in order. Mom had been right about the best way to handle personal questions, I decided.

The tangy scent of meat cooking filled the house when I came home from school that afternoon. All of a sudden my stomach had a hollow sensation, which wasn't surprising as I'd eaten very little since dinner Saturday night before Charlie's final visit.

Mom was in the kitchen, standing by the stove, turning chunks of beef with a long-handled fork. The meat was browning in the bottom of the cast iron Dutch oven which had belonged to *her* mother, and although we had newer pots and pans, there were some foods that she maintained tasted better cooked in the old Dutch oven.

"Smells good," I commented, just to say something.

"I'm making beef stew." She continued to turn the meat so the cooked sides were up and the red sides down. Fat in the bottom of the Dutch oven spattered out and both of us jumped back. I pulled a paper towel from the roller and wiped the grease spot off the floor.

"How was school today?" she asked without taking her eyes off the meat.

"It was all right."

She wanted me to go on, to tell her what happened. I knew it without her having to ask it, and my tongue slid across my dry lips. She continued to turn the pieces of meat until, finally, she gave me a quick look and said, "Did you see Charlie?"

That must have been all I needed to start talking because I began and couldn't stop until I'd related all of it, about seeing Charlie and Wes, then about Charlie avoiding me in the classes we shared and about Karen's questions at lunch. My voice wavered and actually broke a couple of times, but there was a compulsion inside me to describe every agonizing incident.

"This afternoon I didn't walk home the usual way," I admitted. "I came around by Cameron Avenue. It's longer, but I figured Charlie wouldn't take that route home and I wasn't sure I could survive having him ignore me again." I drew a choppy breath. "Mom, thanks for making me go to school. Tomorrow might be awful, but at least I'll know what to expect, and I don't honestly think it could be any more grim than today was."

She patted my arm — something she often did to anyone in the family who was upset — as if just touching would help, and strangely enough, it did.

"I'm proud of the way you're handling this," she said gently. "A crisis of any sort always takes an emotional toll, but the hardest part is behind you now."

Mom poured a cup of hot water into the Dutch oven, fitted the heavy lid into place, and turned the stove burner low. "That can simmer a while before I add the vegetables," she commented.

"I'll fix the vegetables for you," I told her, wanting to keep busy, too busy to think about myself. I also wanted to do some little thing for my mother to show her I was grateful for her understanding.

The potatoes and carrots lay in a loose pile on the counter and the onions were in the grocery store mesh bag, their thin, shiny skins flaking off so that tan wisps fell through the mesh and dotted the countertop. Peeling onions would be great, I mused wryly. That chore always made my eyes water, and the onions could mask the tears that were very near the surface just from the mention of Charlie's name.

chapter
5

My mother was mistaken Monday afternoon when she said the hardest part was behind me. I'm sure she sincerely believed that at the time, and I believed it, too — something I thought about wistfully on Friday, six nights after Charlie had broken up with me.

It seemed strange to be by myself on a Friday night. I wasn't alone in the house — Mom and Dad were in the den — but after dinner I gave the excuse of having to write a book report and went up to my room. Not much was done on the report, though. I was thinking . . . remembering . . .

In the past, sometimes Charlie and I watched TV on Friday nights or played Monopoly in his living room or mine or went to a school dance. On other weekends we were with our friends, seeing movies or eating pizza or going to a party. The best moments of each evening were at the end, and my mouth felt warm with the memory of our good-night kisses.

During that long, long week after Thanksgiving the calendar changed from November to December and my holiday job was to begin the following day, the same job I'd had the previous Christmas holidays. I would be working Saturdays in December and the entire pre-Christmas week after school closed, wrapping packages at the crafts shop where Mom was employed. I'd always liked to put pretty paper and ribbons on presents and it never ceased to amaze me that some people couldn't or wouldn't do their own wrapping. But apparently plenty of folks were all thumbs. Both women and men would come into the shop, their arms loaded with items they'd purchased elsewhere, and pay to have the parcels done up attractively.

It had been a thrill in October when Mrs. Taylor, who owned the handicrafts shop, offered me the wrapping job a second year, but on that first Friday night in December, I wasn't excited about it. Nothing mattered since Charlie turned his back on me. I didn't just miss his embraces and his warm, sweet kisses, but I ached to talk to him, to share his thoughts and tell him mine, to catch his eyes and see his mouth curve into a smile.

At school that week most of my friends gave up trying to get me into conversation, and at home, where I wanted to talk about Charlie because I didn't have to pretend I wasn't hurt, it was like being face-to-face with a brick wall. Mom and Dad apparently felt that the less said, the sooner I'd forget him. They should have known differently. If

I mentioned Charlie's name, they immediately changed the subject.

Nights were the worst time. The gnawing loneliness swirling around me made it hard to concentrate on homework, and at bedtime I was awake when I ought to have been asleep.

Angie returned from Chicago shortly after nine o'clock Wednesday night and telephoned me an hour later as soon as she was in her house.

"Wendy, I can't believe this about you and Charlie!" she gasped. "Wes told me. I wanted to come over tonight, but Dad won't let me because it's late. Wes is in a state of shock about it, too. He said Charlie told him that he wanted to date other girls. I'm so sorry. It must be horrible for you."

"It is. Oh, Angie — "

The words began to tumble out, everything I'd kept bottled up inside. Angie was my closest friend and I could tell her all of it, knowing she'd never betray my confidence. I descibed Charlie's last visit the Saturday before, the way he'd ignored me ever since, and the hurt which cut into me like a sharp knife.

"I don't understand it," I moaned. "I'll never understand."

"I don't, either. Maybe if I talked to Charlie it would help, although I said that to Wes and he thought it was a dumb idea. He said Charlie's mind was made up."

"Maybe you could find out why — if there's a reason Charlie didn't tell me. Angie, I feel so lost, so alone."

"I can imagine. I'd die if Wes did that to me or — Dad is signaling me to ring off, Wendy, so I'd better do it before he gets mad. I'll see you at school tomorrow."

I put the telephone down slowly. A tiny spark of hope flared in me. If Angie could talk to Charlie, if she could explain how I felt, how hurt I was. . . .

I shouldn't have hoped. The next afternoon when she and I were showering after gym she told me Charlie cut her off when she attempted to discuss me. "He wasn't exactly rude," she sighed, "but he made it plain this was between you and him. Wendy, are you all right? You're awfully pale?"

"Sure. I'm fine. As fine as I guess I'll ever be." I zipped my slacks and carefully avoided her eyes while I buttoned my blouse. "I suppose I hoped too much that Charlie would have second thoughts."

"So did I."

Tears were on my lashes and I didn't want to break down, not in the girls' locker room. Angie seemed to sense my feelings as she began rattling on a mile a minute about her trip to Chicago, and by the time the bell rang and we were hurrying to our next classes, I had my emotions in check.

On Thursday evening Helen telephoned from college. She seldom wrote home the year before when she was a freshman, and Mom talked to her about it, eventually telling her to call collect once a week. Helen simply detested writing anything and that included letters. Thursday was the night she and Mom agreed on and the call usually came shortly after seven P.M. when the evening long distance rates went into effect.

Each of us chatted briefly with her and that Thursday when it was my turn, the instant Helen heard my voice she said, "Has Charlie been over? Or have you talked to him at school?"

Gripping the phone hard, I pressed it to my ear as if I wanted to glue it there.

"No . . . uh . . . no," I came back.

"You mean he hasn't said anything?"

"Not except hello." *Don't, Helen. Please, don't,* I begged silently.

"Wendy, you're not just sitting home waiting for him to show up, are you?"

My parents were less than six feet away from where I stood. I would have told Helen the truth except that I couldn't with an audience. Besides, my voice was quivering.

"I have a lot of homework tonight," I replied. "Here's Dad."

"Wait, Wendy! Forget Charlie Peterson — do you hear me? Go out with someone else. Promise you will."

I couldn't promise anything. The lump in my throat felt as big as a hard-boiled egg.

"Here's Dad," I said again and passed the phone to my father.

Helen thought she knew how it felt to be rejected, but she didn't really understand.

Another week inched by, the December days so
short the morning skies were still gray when I left
for school, and the pale, wintry sunshine, which
sometimes appeared later, felt almost as chilled as
the air. I hated the starkness of the barren tree
branches and the stubby, frozen brown grass in
neighborhood yards. Even the evergreens had taken
on a rusty drabness that matched my mood.

Charlie was dating.

Maybe he had been seeing girls regularly since
the Saturday after Thanksgiving, but it wasn't
obvious enough for me to know about it until the
middle of December. He and I spoke when we
passed at school; his "Wendy" was an acknowledg-
ment that I was in view although he never said
more than my name. I would feel my mouth as dry
as sandpaper and by the time I managed "Hello"
he had moved on, out of hearing.

He ate lunch with Suzanne Howard two days in

succession, while I died slowly in my chair across the cafeteria. He spoke to me without actually looking at me coming out of English class one morning, then ambled over to Karen and put his arm through hers, both of them laughing as if they shared a secret joke.

That hurt. I caught my breath and hurried down the hall, my eyes misting with tears. It was like a knife turning in my heart to see Charlie with a girl, especially with one of my friends, and Karen was *supposed* to be my friend. I wouldn't have done that to her if our places had been reversed. She and Danny Brooks must have broken up since I spotted him giving a lot of attention to a senior, Natalie Gorman. I probably could have asked Angie about Charlie, but it still hurt too much to say his name aloud.

As for me, I'd become a hermit, keeping to myself at school and rejecting Angie's pleas for me to go to the movies with her and Wes or to let her ask Wes to line up a date for me. It seemed impossible for her to grasp the fact that I didn't want to be with any boy except Charlie.

My mother couldn't understand, either. I began avoiding conversations with her. If she was at home when I came in from school, I gave her a quick greeting and headed to the privacy of my room. As soon as the dinner dishes were done, I went upstairs once more.

That's how things were when Mom and I had an ugly confrontation.

My mother was a fabulously well-organized individual, especially at Christmas. Knowing she would be working extra hours at the shop during December, she always bought her gifts early in the fall and wrapped them immediately. By mid-November the cards she and Dad were sending had been addressed and stamped and were in a box on her closet shelf, ready to be taken to the post office. One year Helen and I teased her, telling her she couldn't get the true Christmas spirit if she wasn't in a last-minute rush, and she laughed, saying that she was thankful "not to be as much of a slowpoke as you two turtles."

The Christmas season had always been special to me. I enjoyed bustling around stores in throngs of people, and a lot of planning went into selecting gifts. Every year I looked forward to bringing the tree decorations down from the attic, and even when I was just twelve or thirteen I begged to be allowed to tie the perky red velvet bow on the front door wreath. During the holidays Mom, Helen, and I took cookies to a nearby nursing home and the spicy smell of those cookies baking was as much a part of my festivities as singing carols and going to church at midnight on Christmas Eve.

At least, it had been that way in the past.

After Charlie and I broke up, I tried very hard to tune Christmas out of my thoughts. In the crafts shop on Saturdays, I had to force myself to smile at the customers, a mechanical smile which might just as well have been painted on a department store mannequin. My hands were busy with colored wrappings and shiny ribbon, and the radio filled every corner with songs about holly and red-nosed reindeer, but I could only feel sadness. Charlie had always been involved in my Christmas, and now, he was gone.

That was what led to the bad scene with Mom. She followed me upstairs one afternoon in the middle of December and asked me point-blank if I'd finished Christmas shopping. I'm positive she already knew the answer.

"No, I haven't," I answered and dropped my school books on the desk.

"Have you begun shopping, Wendy?"

The second "No" was a whisper. *Couldn't she leave me alone? Didn't she have anything better to do than badger me?*

"Wendy, if you need some money—"

"I'll have enough money." I spoke flatly, almost in a harsh tone, hoping she would take the hint and realize I wasn't in the mood to chat.

Instead, she gave a long sigh. "Just when do you plan to start getting ready for Christmas?" she persisted. "The merchandise in the stores is picked over now and next Monday you'll start working at the shop full-time with school closed. You ought—"

"I'll do it when I'm good and ready and not before so just shut up!" I cut in, the words tumbling out furiously. "Can't you get off my back, Mom? I'm not in diapers anymore—or haven't you noticed? You don't have to remind me Christmas is coming and if you're so afraid *you* won't get a lot of presents, I'll see that you have a pile under the tree if it's the last thing I ever do! But just quit nagging me! I despise being hounded all the time!"

Her eyes opened very wide, and she clamped her lips together without speaking. I was stunned at what I'd just said because she hadn't been nagging or hounding me, and I could not believe I'd uttered those hateful remarks to my mother. It was embarrassing to look at her.

A sudden, eerie silence filled the room.

"Mom," I whispered, "I'm sorry. I didn't mean . . ." My voice trailed off.

The telephone rang. She brushed past me and went across the hall to her bedroom where the extension phone was. I heard her say, "Yes, Wendy is here," in a strained tone.

I didn't want to speak to anyone, but I didn't want to face my mother, either. When I took the phone from Mom, Angie was on the line. She couldn't have chosen a worse time to call.

"Wendy, I'm inviting some of the school gang over Friday night," she said. "I hope you'll come."

"Thanks, but no thanks," I muttered thinly.

"Please don't refuse until you hear what I have to say. If you're concerned about being in the same room with Charlie, I simply won't include him and if he gets mad — so what? You really ought to get out, Wendy. You don't need a date for Friday night unless you want one. I'll ask Wes to pick you up on his way here, and he and I will drive you home."

"I . . . I can't, Angie. I just can't."

"That's a negative attitude. You — "

"I have to go now," I interrupted her and hung up without saying good-bye.

Mom had returned to my room and was sitting by the desk, obviously waiting for me. "Did Angie want you to go somewhere?" she asked.

"She's having a crowd over."

"I heard you tell her no. You can't stay home and mope forever, Wendy."

My lips felt tight as if I'd been outdoors in a cold wind. The silence seemed to exasperate my mother and she got up abruptly, prowling around the room. When she spoke again, her irritation showed.

"I've been sympathetic with you — until now," she snapped. "I know you've been hurt, Wendy, and it's harder than you realize for me to watch you suffer. Hard for your father, too. But it's time for you to accept what happened. Charlie has made a definite break and he's not going to date you again — not any time soon. You've spent long enough wallowing in self-pity, and you aren't helping your own situation by this poor-little-me attitude. That's only part of it, though. You're making everyone around you wretched."

My knees felt wobbly and I sat down on the side of the bed. I had the impression Mom was waiting for me to make some kind of reply, and I couldn't.

"You are ruining our family life, whether you're conscious of it or not," she went on. "Helen will be coming in Friday and I won't have you spoiling her holidays even if you're determined to spoil your own. Feeling sorry for yourself at first was natural, but doing it for days and weeks becomes selfish, regardless of your being hurt. Frankly, Wendy, I'm amazed Angie wants you at her party if you've acted as coldly toward her as you've been to your father and me."

"Mom, you don't understand."

"I understand much more than you think. I've

47

been hoping it wouldn't be necessary to say these things to you, but there isn't any other way. You're being inconsiderate and childish, Wendy. It doesn't make *you* feel any better, and that's the best reason for you to make a real effort to snap out of it. At the same time, you're not thinking about a soul but yourself."

I gasped at the sudden realization that she was right. An unfamiliar sensation made my chest feel as if something was giving way, as if my heart had been encased in ice, and now the ice was starting to melt.

"But I don't know what to do," I moaned. "It hurts to think about Charlie. It hurts so much I feel like I'll die from the pain. And I can't stop thinking about him."

Her face softened and she came to me, taking a seat beside me on the bed and covering my hands with hers. "The first thing for you to do is to get rid of everything in your room that keeps Charlie in your thoughts," she said gently. "The pictures. Those stuffed rabbits. The — "

"Mom, I can't," I cut in, picking up the blue rabbit and cradling it against my breast. "I can't do that."

"Yes, you can. And you must. Put the rabbits away this afternoon and tonight I'll go over to the shopping center with you and you can get a new stuffed animal so your bed won't seem bare."

My arms tightened around the rabbit, and I ducked my head because I was almost crying and didn't want Mom to know. I guess she'd already noticed the tears on my lashes.

"You don't have to throw away the things Charlie gave you," she said. "Your time with him has been an important phase of your life, and I hope eventually you'll be able to enjoy looking at the snapshots and the gifts he gave you and remembering the fun you had with him. But at the moment, that's impossible. The best solution is to have these reminders of him out of sight."

She paused. I clung to the rabbit.

"Wendy, another thing you must do is to make yourself be with your friends," she added. "It may be difficult for you at first, and you'll have to brace yourself for seeing Charlie with other girls, but the sooner you do it, the sooner you can get back to normal and start to enjoy life again."

"I've already seen him with girls at school. I know he must be dating."

"You're a sensible person, dear. You're kind and thoughtful by nature, and I'm sure, if you stop to think about it, you'd never deliberately upset the people who care about you. So, don't behave that way now. Being sour and bitter can become a habit, and you're too lovely a girl to allow that to happen to you."

I hadn't thought about the danger of slipping into being permanently disagreeable. The idea was terrifying. In my misery, I'd been wrapped up in myself. *My* pain. *My* loneliness. *My* heartache. Mom was prejudiced where I was concerned, by saying I was sensible, kind, and lovely. Other people wouldn't be that tolerant, and it hadn't occurred to me that simply because I was suffering, I might be punishing my family and my friends.

"Mom, I guess you're right," I said in a shaky voice.

"Your father and I love you very much."

"You can love me even after the terrible things I said to you a little while ago?"

"Oh, that." She shrugged and smiled. "You forget it. I already have."

She was fibbing, of course, to make me feel better. She couldn't forget it any more than I could, but I knew what she meant, that she'd forgiven me for my hateful remarks. I wished with all my heart I could retract them. I had wanted to hurt her because what she was telling me about myself was a hundred percent true, and it wasn't pleasant to hear.

Mom went to the kitchen to begin preparing dinner, refusing my offer of help. I sat on the bed a long time, watching the afternoon fade into a lavender twilight, seeing the street lamps come on, ignoring the shadows in my room. Despite the closed windows, the rumble of rush-hour traffic sounded from the next street, which was a main thoroughfare. Car doors banged nearby, an indication some of our neighbors were coming home from work.

There was plenty of time for me to think. *I won't spoil Christmas for the family,* I vowed silently. *I'll smile and pretend to be happy.*

I couldn't go to Angie's get-together, though. Not yet.

After a while I crossed the hall to my parents' room and telephoned Angie. "I'm sorry I hung up on you," I told her. "Thanks for the invitation and for offering not to include Charlie, but he's your friend the same as I am. It isn't right for you to have to choose between us or for him to be cut out of a fun evening. Besides, Helen is coming from college Friday, and I'd hate to be away on her first night here. I'll be at your next party whether Charlie is there or not, though." I said all of it hurriedly. If I'd paused once, my throat might have closed up.

"Okay," she answered. "I'll hold you to the next one. Maybe I'll have another party real soon.

"See you at school tomorrow, Angie."

"Sure. Thanks for calling. Good-bye for now."

My good-bye was loud and clear that time, and I let her ring off first.

It seemed odd for Angie and me to have such a quick telephone conversation because under other circumstances we'd have gabbed for an hour—or until her parents or mine made us stop. Maybe she was annoyed with me because of my comments when she phoned, or maybe she could tell I was too upset to continue.

There wasn't any point in delaying what had to be done. I went to the attic for one of the empty cardboard boxes stored there and packed it with everything having to do with Charlie. The two rabbits were the last to go in, their glass eyes glittering in the reflection from the overhead light fixture.

My room looked uncomfortably naked with so much removed. I would get a couple of posters to use for decorations, I decided, and if Mom took me shopping for a new stuffed animal, I'd choose a yellow or a white one. A kangaroo or a kitten or a bear. Something very different from the pink and blue rabbits.

For a moment I considered putting the box in

my closet, but if it stayed within easy reach, the temptation to open it occasionally would be tremendous. Choking back a sigh, I lugged it to the attic and left it in a corner between the high chair Helen and I used when we were small and an old cabinet radio that hadn't worked in ages.

chapter
7

Christmas morning at our house was the same
year after year — Dad claimed it was proof that
we'd created our own traditions. For breakfast
there was stollen, a German coffee cake dotted with
candied cherries, and as soon as we ate we trooped
to the living room to open gifts. Afterwards, while
my mother was getting the turkey stuffed and into
the oven, Dad built a fire on the den hearth and
Helen set the dining room table with a bright red
cloth and the best china. I made beds and gathered
up the mountain of torn tissue paper from the living
room floor.

In the past, that was about the time Charlie
arrived.

I made a big effort not to think about Charlie
although my eyes misted when Helen opened three
packages from Stan. It wasn't that I craved presents
from Charlie. I just longed to see him, to be with
him. *Cut it out, Wendy Scott!* I ordered myself

sharply. To get my thoughts away from memories, I tried on the beautiful pale aqua sweater Mom had knitted for me. She worked on it when I wasn't around so it would be a Christmas surprise, she said.

Mr. and Mrs. Cameron, who lived next door, were invited every year for Christmas dinner since they had no family in the area and no children. Another of our holiday traditions was eating at two in the afternoon instead of having dinner at night. Mom outdid herself with the meal, and Helen and I made short work of the dishes since she was expecting Stan.

My parents and the Camerons settled themselves in front of the den fire, laughing and chatting; Helen went out with Stan to meet a group of friends. I headed upstairs for lack of anything more interesting to do, determined not to permit myself to feel pitiful, not on Christmas Day.

I was restless, though. I suppose I could have contacted Angie, but she probably was with Wes, and no doubt Karen had plans. Boys constantly flocked around Karen and I'd be more than ever like the proverbial fifth wheel.

Going to see Patti Simms was a spur-of-the-moment idea. I'm not sure what made me think of her, except that I wanted to get out of the house and vaguely remembered Patti mentioning in the school cafeteria that her family was moving to my street, Hawthorne.

Patti was quiet and studious, the sort of girl everybody described as "nice," and she didn't seem to go out with any boys. Conversation with Patti wouldn't be about social activities and she was too polite to ask prying questions about Charlie Peterson.

Her house number escaped me, although it was in the 2900 block. I recalled thinking at the time she mentioned the move that she would be fifteen blocks further from school than I was at 1402 Hawthorne. Fifteen blocks to Patti's and another fifteen back would make quite a walk, I mused Christmas afternoon as I got into my coat. Still, the distance offered me a valid excuse not to linger at Patti's more than half an hour in order to be home before dark.

The air was cold despite the bright sun, and the wind was blustery enough to make my cheeks tingle. I deliberately kept my eyes straight ahead as I went past the Petersons' house, refusing to wonder what I'd do if Charlie should come out at that precise moment. It didn't happen. Farther along, two little boys were pulling a brand-new sled across their lawn — although there wasn't a speck of snow; a block later a girl who was about six was wobbling on a shiny red bike which had training wheels. She was smiling and I smiled, too, remembering how excited I was the year I got my first big bike.

Locating Patti's house in the 2900 block was no problem as "Simms" was painted on the mailbox. It was a white clapboard split-level with blue shutters, and Patti opened the door.

"Wendy!" she gasped, her eyebrows lifting in amazement. "What are you doing here?"

She was astonished since I'd never visited her before. At that moment I felt like a freak. Nobody went to see a casual acquaintance uninvited on Christmas afternoon. That was a time reserved for family and close friends.

"I . . . uh . . . thought I'd drop over," I said hesitantly. "With my job during the holidays and . . .

and everything, I haven't welcomed you to the neighborhood."

Still obviously surprised, she invited me in. For the first time, I realized she had on a coat.

"You must be going out," I said.

"Just to my grandparents' apartment for dinner. Mama — " she turned to an older woman who joined us. Mrs. Simms also had on a coat plus a fuzzy woollen tam. "Mama, this is Wendy Scott and she just got here. Do we have to go to Grandma's right now? Couldn't we wait a little while? Please."

"Your grandmother will be very upset if we're late because we'd hold up dinner for the other guests," Mrs. Simms said to Patti. Her next remark was for me. "Wendy, I hope you understand, and that you'll come again soon."

Patti looked as if she was about to cry with disappointment which made me think her Christmas hadn't been any more exciting than mine. I assured both of them I'd be back soon and stepped outside once more.

During that brief time with Patti the sun had dropped from sight behind the houses lining the west side of Hawthorne Street. Night was coming faster than I'd anticipated, the faint rosy sunset colors already changing to smoky gray, and now the wind was tinged with ice. I realized I'd been stupid to attempt that long a walk so near dusk. No doubt Mom and Dad would read me the riot act when I reached home — they'd warned me many times about being alone on the street after dark.

A few cars moved on Hawthorne, their headlights slicing into the shadows. No pedestrians were in view — except me. I hurried, taking such long strides I was panting.

A blue automobile passed, then slowed and the driver backed up until he was beside me. My heart pounded like a bongo drum and a panicky sensation made my mouth gritty. I continued to walk ignoring the blue sedan, deliberately not turning my head toward it.

"Hey, Wendy! Wendy Scott!" a male voice rang out.

The sound of my name made me whirl around. Mark Thompson was behind the steering wheel with his twin brother, Alan, beside him. Like me, they were juniors at Roosevelt High School although I knew them only casually.

"Isn't it kind of a nippy night for a stroll?" Alan asked. "Want a ride?"

"Do I ever!" I almost collapsed with relief at the realization that the car was filled with people I knew.

Alan got out so I could slide in between them. The car heater gave forth a blast of warm air.

"Ooooooh, that feels good," I said, taking off my gloves and holding my hands to the heater. "I was freezing. You two are a lifesaver."

"Correction," Mark grinned. "We're lifesavers with an s. Just because we're twins doesn't mean you can lump us into a glob."

"I never thought about the problems twins have," I said. "You two look so much alike — "

"Correction again," Alan interrupted. "I'm handsome. He's just your ordinary creep."

I laughed out loud. The boys were identical twins, both stockily built with dark hair and eyes.

I wouldn't have been able to tell them apart except that Alan had a small scar above his left eyebrow. It wasn't disfiguring, just a thin, pale line about an inch long.

It dawned on me I hadn't laughed like that in ages. Not since Thanksgiving.

"Where are you heading, Wendy?" Mark asked.

"Home. That's 1402 Hawthorne. What about you two?"

"For starters, we thought we'd ride past Mallory's Doughnut Shop to see what's left after the fire," Alan answered.

"Fire? What fire?" Mallory's was near Roosevelt High, and lots of kids stopped there for snacks after school. Charlie and I had eaten doughnuts there many times.

"You mustn't have had your radio or TV tuned to a news program today," Alan said. "Mallory's burned this afternoon."

I wanted to see how much damage the fire caused, so Mark zipped past my house. Mallory's was a disaster. Only twisted steel supports were standing and a thin, smoky haze hung over the charred debris. The putrid smell of burned grease and sugar was awful. Somebody had roped off the area, and the street lamps illuminated a cardboard sign that said NO TRESPASSING in square orange letters.

Other people were gazing at what once had been the doughnut shop, and several cars stopped in the street. Someone yelled to the Thompson twins, and I recognized Jeff Bryant, a boy I knew casually at school.

"Hi, Wendy," Jeff added, as if he was surprised to find me with Alan and Mark.

"Poor Mr. Mallory," I sighed. "I hope he had insurance."

"Enough insurance to rebuild," Jeff commented.

"Enough insurance to rebuild on the same spot in a hurry," Alan grinned. "Some days the only thing that gets me through my last period class is the thought of a hot doughnut."

All of us laughed. Jeff said, "See you around," and returned to his car. The Thompsons and I got into the front seat of theirs, and Mark continued to drive. Alan slid one arm along the back of the car seat, not actually putting it around me although I was aware of his fingers brushing my shoulder ever so slightly.

"Wendy, I hope you aren't rushing to go home?" Alan said. It was a question rather than a statement.

Not knowing what he was thinking, I wasn't sure how to reply. My house was in sight. I could see Mom at the living room window, her hands cupped around her eyes as she peered out. I hadn't told her I was going anywhere when I left for Patti's, and it was easy to guess she was concerned about me.

All of the sudden I realized I didn't want to go in and have Mark and Alan drive away. Being with them had been fun, nicer than sitting in my room alone. I didn't want to *date* any boy but Charlie, but continuing the evening with the twins couldn't be classified as a "date" since there were two of them. In that split second another thought crystallized in my brain: lately I'd given my mother a hard time, and she would be happy to see me with some friends.

Mark had his foot on the brake. Alan was looking at me, waiting for my answer.

"I'm not really in a hurry," I said, stalling for time. "My mother is expecting me, though."

"Couldn't you check in with her and explain that you're going with us? Mark and I plan to grab some burgers for supper and if you'll come along, you'll save me from being trapped with *him*." Alan jerked his head good-naturedly toward his brother.

"Yeah, Wendy," Mark urged. "Come along."

I amazed myself with what I said next because the words weren't planned. "Hamburgers on Christmas night? That's got to be a no-no." I glanced from one of the twins to the other and laughed. "Maybe it's even against the law not to have turkey sandwiches Christmas night. Besides, I'll bet all the hamburger places are closed. We have half a turkey and two kinds of dessert left from dinner, so if you want to make your own sandwiches — "

"It's a deal!" Mark didn't let me finish. With a quick movement he flipped off the ignition and the headlights.

"You sure don't have to coax me," Alan said softly and smiled. That time his fingers touched my shoulder. In fact, he gave me a quick squeeze.

If my parents were surprised to have me bring two boys in for supper, they hid their feelings and no questions were asked. Later I told Mom about going to see Patti and the Thompsons offering me a ride.

Dad said he was glad to have another opportunity to use the new electric carving knife Helen had given him, and he cut a huge pile of turkey slices.

My mother brought out a loaf of bread and what remained of the mince pie and lemon cake. She poured milk for Alan, while I made a pot of tea for Mark and myself. My parents went back to the den when the twins and I sat down at the kitchen table.

We talked about school at first — a lot of crazy remarks were tossed back and forth, with the boys enough at ease for me to relax. After a time the conversation became more serious because of a casual comment Alan made about food.

"Wendy, you must be right about having turkey for Christmas," he said as he made himself a second sandwich. "I really feel like it's Christmas now. Otherwise, it's been just any other day except for unwrapping packages this morning."

"I guess food depends on your traditions," I murmured. "Some people prefer ham or have a goose or roast beef for Christmas."

"Or TV dinners," Mark said sarcastically. "That seems to be our current family tradition. Not that Dad, Alan, or I go for the arrangement, but it's the way it is since Mom redecorated the house. My mother goes into orbit if anybody uses the kitchen except to boil water or pour cereal out of a box."

Mark sounded too bitter to be kidding. Not use the kitchen? What was a kitchen for if it wasn't to be used? It dawned on me I didn't know much about the twins as they'd gone to a different grammar school and junior high. Since the three of us had been at Roosevelt, I'd seen them at ball games and school functions, but nowhere else except class.

During the brief silence which followed, Alan

gave his brother a scorching look. Mark's forehead turned dark red. "That wasn't meant to be as much of a slam as it probably seemed," Mark muttered.

Alan's annoyance continued to show. I tried to think of another topic to talk about and my mind went blank.

"Mom has an interior decorating business, and her office and shop are in our house," Mark continued. "It's actually kind of a family affair as Dad does the bookkeeping on weekends — he's an accountant — and Alan and I pitch in to unpack crates and keep the samples in order. But Mom wants everything shiny and on display so when her clients come in they can see how a house is supposed to look. Nothing can get messed up, not even on holidays and Sundays, and that goes double for the kitchen. You know how kitchens look in magazine pictures, Wendy? Well, that's ours."

"She really likes helping people choose wallpaper and rugs and stuff," Alan chimed in, as if he wanted to defend his mother. "Mom's okay."

Alan and Mark appeared uncomfortable and I imagined they wished nothing had been said about their family life. I managed to change the subject, and we weren't serious again until a couple of hours later when they were ready to leave. They made a point of going into the den to thank Mom and Dad for the food.

As the guys reached my front door, Alan said, "Wendy, how about a movie tomorrow night?"

"I . . . I . . ." Remembering that I didn't want to date any boy but Charlie, a refusal was on the tip of my tongue. Then I changed my mind. I wasn't sure why; it just happened.

"Sounds like fun," I answered.

"Would you rather see the early show or the second one?" Mark asked.

"Hey — stow it, Mark!" Alan barked. "*I* invited Wendy! You bug off!"

They looked daggers at each other.

"The three of us can — " I started.

"No, the three of us can't!" Alan broke in, still glaring at Mark. "If my brother wants a date, let him find his own girl!"

The silence was awesome. I don't suppose it lasted more than half a minute although it was endless to me. Mark muttered, "Good night, Wendy. Thanks for the swell time."

He opened the front door and stepped outside. A surge of icy air came into the house. The porch light was on and I could see Mark through the glass panes in the door, his shoulders hunched up and his back very stiff. I didn't want him to leave angry. Or for Alan to be mad, either.

"If Mark gets a date we can double for the movie tomorrow night," I suggested hopefully, my voice low so Mark wouldn't overhear.

"He won't. He's shy with girls."

"He didn't act shy tonight, Alan, and I'm a girl."

"Tonight he was shy at first. He didn't want to stop and offer you a ride until I insisted. He doesn't date. Oh, he's been around girls, but he wouldn't even invite a girl to the prom last spring or to the school mixer last September. I don't know if he's scared a girl will turn him down or what. As I just said to him, though, *I'm* the one who asked you for a date tomorrow night. Of course, if you're trying to say you don't want to go with me . . ." The sentence hung there, unfinished.

"I *do* want to go to the movies with you. It's just that I don't enjoy seeing another person unhappy. What if I find a date for Mark?"

"Well . . . if you want to do that, it's okay, I guess. You'd better ask him about it."

I reached for the doorknob, but Alan stopped me my touching my wrist. He didn't hold it. He merely touched it enough to make me draw my hand back from the knob and I looked up at him.

"Wait a minute, Wendy," he said. "Maybe we should get something straight. How is it with you and Charlie Peterson?"

If he had hit me, I wouldn't have been more startled. Alan's features blurred before my eyes and it was difficult to breathe, impossible to answer him at once.

"I'm not digging into your business," he added. "But if I'm stepping on some other guy's territory, I want to know about it."

"Charlie and I are . . . are friends," I said thickly.

I'd spoken Charlie's name! I'd actually said "Charlie" aloud and I hadn't cried.

The tension went out of Alan and he smiled as he pulled the door open. He and I went outside to where Mark was waiting. I shivered in the cold, thankful for the fact that the two boys were staring at each other instead of at me. I wasn't sure how composed I was.

Mark seemed eager when I offered to get a date for him — his "Sure, Wendy. Great," came in a natural tone. The two of them started for their car, and I hurried indoors.

I wouldn't permit myself to think about Charlie until I'd said good night to Mom and Dad and was in my room. Undressing quickly, I crawled into bed and pulled the stuffed kitten into the crook of my elbow. That kitten was what my mother bought for me to replace Charlie's two rabbits.

Charlie, I thought wistfully, wondering if he had enjoyed his Christmas. I wondered if he'd thought about me at all? Whether I mattered to him even a tiny bit now? And if he'd remembered the other holidays when we were together?

My room was in the front of the house and when an automobile stopped outside, its headlights put a quick flash of yellow across the wall over my desk. I sat up in bed to look out and recognized Helen and Stan as they left the car and came up the walk, his arm around her waist.

The corner streetlight shone diagonally through our yard, but there was one spot at the foot of the porch steps — the kissing spot, Charlie used to call it — where low branches of a cedar tree swept the ground and cast a shadow. Helen and Stan stopped in that dark cedar circle and stood very close together. He bent his head and I knew they were kissing.

I lay down again, clutching the kitten, embarrassed at spying on them although it wasn't done intentionally. A hard lump rose into my throat. Charlie used to kiss me in the cedar shadow every time we came in or went out of the house after dark. I wanted him so much my heart ached.

chapter
8

At eleven o'clock the next morning I telephoned
Patti about going to the movies with Mark, Alan,
and me. I was in an apprehensive frame of mind.
My self-confidence had vanished overnight, and I
wondered why I accepted a date with Alan when I
yearned for Charlie. In the morning sunshine I
wished I hadn't offered so glibly to fix Mark up for
the evening. I couldn't think of another girl to ask
if Patti refused.

Neither Mark nor Patti were used to dating, and
they might not hit it off. With both of them shy, I
visualized long silences — or their filling the time
with the forced chitchat that was almost as painful.
Yet, Patti was the only girl I knew who might be
free and wouldn't mind being asked on such short
notice. At least, I hoped she wouldn't. Mark wasn't
actually a blind date since she knew him at school,
although most girls would feel insulted if the guy

didn't do his own phoning under those circumstances.

Patti said, "Oh, I'd love it! I'd just adore going out tonight! Thanks so much, Wendy. The Thompson twins seem awfully nice. That is, the little I know them. Which one is Mark? With the scar or without it?"

"Without. I have to dash now. See you tonight, Patti." As I rang off I hoped she could keep some of that animation until night. If she clammed up the way she normally did with boys, the evening would be difficult.

I'd been using the den phone and Helen, who was still in her pajamas, came in with a mug of coffee and flopped on the couch. She had overheard most of my conversation with Patti.

"Sounds as if you've finally come out of your cave, Wendy," she said when I returned the phone to its cradle. "Mom told me you had a date last night. I hope that means you've gotten around to closing the file on Charlie."

"It was *not* a date," I answered stiffly. "Two friends came in and they happened to be male."

"Why are you acting so defensive? I think it's great. Are you seeing those male friends again any time soon?"

She put extra emphasis on the word male. Helen knew my plans. She'd taken in every word I said to Patti, and a feeling of irritation came over me. Sisters, I reflected darkly, could be the very devil at times.

"I'm going to the movies tonight with Alan Thompson and we're doubling with his brother and

Patti Simms, the girl I just called." I said it in the ultra-patient voice you'd use to explain something to a child, figuring Helen would get the message and hush. It was a stupid assumption on my part.

"It's past time you got Charlie out of your system," she continued. "I'll bet he hasn't been sitting mooning over you."

"Helen! Lay off!" I shouted. "Do we have to discuss me? With both of us having jobs before Christmas and you seeing Stan every night, you and I have scarcely had a glimpse of one another since you came home, but whenever we've been in the same room, you start in on Charlie and me! I'm fed to the teeth with it! Can't we take a breather on that subject?"

She looked flustered. I'll have to give her that. I was embarrassed because I remembered how Mom told me disagreeableness could become a habit — and I wasn't being pleasant.

Helen set her coffee mug on the table by the couch. "I didn't realize . . . I mean . . . Okay, maybe I have come on strong, Wendy. But I wasn't conscious of it. Anyhow, it's a relief to know you're dating because that's a sign you're returning to the Land of the Living."

I let my breath out slowly and tried to smile at her, sure any further discussion of Charlie Peterson was over for that particular day. Once again, I was mistaken. The Charlie-Wendy thing appeared to be everybody's favorite topic.

When Mom came home from the shop she said I could use her car, and in the middle of the afternoon I went over to Angie's. Admiring each other's gifts was a post-Christmas routine for us. She looked at the car and laughingly commented that we must have grown up at last — when we were younger we rode our bikes between the two houses.

Wes had given Angie a gold bracelet and a luscious cream-colored canvas pocketbook trimmed with bands of brown leather. She beamed when I said they were beautiful.

"I think so, too," she agreed and held her arm up so the sun's rays shimmered on the bracelet. "He spent too much. I told him that last night, but he claims I'm worth it."

A familiar tightness filled my chest. There was a time when I would have told Charlie he was spending too much on my presents. Now, I was silent.

Angie looked straight at me. "Did you hear from Charlie yesterday?" she asked.

"Was I supposed to hear from him?" Answering a question with a question is a dodge to keep from giving a real reply.

"I just wondered, Wendy. I thought he might have sent you a small gift. Something friendly rather than real personal."

"Why should he?" I was on the defensive again. "I certainly didn't expect to hear from him, and I didn't send him anything."

"You're irked because I asked, Wendy. I can always tell when you're starting to get mad. Your nostrils quiver."

"Who gave you the blue stationery?" I inquired, ignoring what she'd said about me.

"My aunt in Boston. Listen, Karen and I thought we'd do something tonight. I don't know exactly what. Maybe go to the concert in town. I was going to phone you about it. Why don't you come with us?"

"Ask me some other time. I — "

"Honestly, you're impossible!" she blurted out, not waiting for me to finish. "You make me angry, Wendy! Aren't you tired of giving your friends the ice water treatment? You don't have to be afraid you'll see Charlie tonight, if that's what's on your mind, because he'll be at the bowling alley."

"I can't go with you and Karen tonight because I have a date." I made my voice as casual as possible. Oddly enough, I felt almost smug. It was good to have a legitimate reason to refuse, proof that my personal situation was under control. At least, that's what I wanted her to believe.

"A date? With whom? You never told me you were dating! You never even hinted at it! Wendy, don't keep me in suspense! Who is he?"

She was so pleased that I laughed. "It isn't the event of the century," I came back, enjoying her curiosity. "We're going to the movies, not getting married."

"But who is he?"

"Who just said what about somebody getting mad?" I teased. "My nostrils can't compare to your eyebrows. Your eyebrows are actually twitching."

"Wendy, who — ?"

"Alan Thompson."

I've heard of people being speechless from surprise, but until that moment, I hadn't seen it happen. Angie opened her mouth, her lips forming a circle, puckering like she was ready to blow out a candle. And not a word came from her.

The stunned expression on her face unnerved me, and for the third time that day I was on the defensive. "Alan asked me and he's an okay person," I murmured.

"He sure is. I'm glad, Wendy. Truly. Everybody has been worried about you, including me. I can imagine how awful I'd feel if Wes dropped me flat the way Charlie did you."

"I guess there's been plenty of gossip about it, huh?"

"Some people will gab about anything." She shrugged, barely pausing for breath before saying, "Tell me about you and Alan. How long have you been dating him? What's he like?"

"I can't tell you what he's like until tomorrow."

"So this is your first date with him? I never heard of Mark going with a girl, but I know Alan dates because one night about a month ago Wes and I sat several rows behind him at the movies. He was with a girl. I didn't see her face. To tell the truth, I didn't pay any attention to them because the movie was good."

I murmured, "Oh," and Angie kept talking.

"Remember the date Alan brought to the fall mixer in the gym last September?" she asked. "The gorgeous blonde? He introduced her to Wes and me when we were standing at the refreshment table and her name was Barbara or Bonnie — something beginning with the letter B because I thought at the time she had three B's. Beautiful, blond, Barbara — or whatever."

"Have you seen her at Roosevelt?"

Angie shook her head. "I guess she goes to another high school. Alan was radiant."

It appeared that Alan Thompson knew lots of girls. I had no recollection of the "gorgeous blonde" at the fall mixer because that September night my eyes had been on Charlie and no one else. I knew exactly the way Charlie looked that evening.

"You didn't tell me how you and Alan got together," Angie went on.

After hearing about Alan's other dates, the last thing I wanted was to admit my Christmas meeting with him was accidental. I didn't lie; what I told Angie wasn't the entire tale, though.

"He asked if I'd like to go to the movies and I said yes," I murmured.

"Just like that! Boom-boom-boom — good and fast. I think it's really romantic."

"A movie date — romantic? You're nuts, Angie."

"I feel like hugging him for talking you into going out."

"Watch it!" I found myself giggling the way Angie and I always giggled when we tossed silly comments at each other. "Alan is my date for tonight, not yours. You give your hugs to someone else."

chapter
9

I was the shy one that night.

Not Patti or Mark. Not Alan. *Me.* My brain must not have been functioning, because I barely managed a comment about anything the first half of the evening.

My horrible apprehension started while I was dressing. Clothes had nothing to do with it as mine were all right — gray slacks with a white shirt and the new aqua sweater Mom knitted. But I looked at my reflection in the mirror and thought about the gorgeous blonde Alan had dated, and all of a sudden my legs were like wet spaghetti.

My light brown hair was shiny clean and my eyes were as blue as ever and my nose turned up a little, just as it always had, but for some unknown reason I didn't feel the least bit pretty. The weird part is that I had never thought about it much before. In the past, I was happy and it showed. Sometimes I'd even sparkled — back then.

73

Now, I felt unloved and that showed, too. Oh, sure, my family loved me and perhaps friends did, but the boy I loved no longer loved me.

"Wendy, Alan is here," Mom called from downstairs.

Fresh worries churned inside of me. I'd never been out with a boy except Charlie, not for a real date, and I didn't know what to say . . . how to act . . . Would Alan try to kiss me? Should I let him do it? Would he get mad if I didn't? What if he wanted more than a good-night kiss?

"Alan is here," Mom called again. In a lower voice she said, "I don't think Wendy heard me the first time or she'd have answered," a remark apparently addressed to Alan.

My "Coming right now" reverberated through the house. I sprayed on perfume and forced the corners of my mouth into what I hoped was a natural-looking smile.

At the car Alan indicated he and I would sit in front. Mark, alone on the backseat, appeared as ill at ease as I felt.

"Wendy, if you want to know why Mark drove yesterday and I'm driving now, it's because today is my day," Alan explained. "The morning Dad turned this car over to us, Mark and I had a big argument about which one would drive. The old man played Solomon and said we'd flip a coin in the beginning and after that, we were to alternate days. We're still alternating. Sometimes it's darned inconvenient if we aren't going in the same direction, but it sure keeps down trouble."

"I drive tomorrow," Mark said. "Who is my date, Wendy?"

"Patti Simms."

Neither boy spoke. I mentioned her address as Alan pulled the car away from my house.

I tried frantically to think of something to say and couldn't even comment on the weather. The silence in the car was gruesome. Glancing over my shoulder at Mark, I saw his expression hadn't changed. There was no way for me to tell if he was disappointed or pleased. Alan seemed intent on his driving. Too intent. It didn't make sense for us to have been talkative and comfortable in my kitchen Christmas night and now, twenty-four hours later, to act like strangers. *Say something, say something*, I ordered myself. Mercifully, the Simmses' house was in sight and I didn't have to do it.

Alan suggested that the three of us go to the door and Mark gave a speedy, "Good idea!" I figured the boys had planned it before they stopped for me. Patti turned out to be the surprise. She looked cute in a short, dark green coat and a green plaid skirt; it may have been excitement or nervousness, but she began to chatter the instant she saw us and continued all the way to the theater. What she said wasn't earth-shaking, but she was bright and animated which was more than could be said for me.

During the movie, which I only half-watched, I decided on some conversation subjects for the ride home in case my mind went blank again. I'd find out if the boys had after-school jobs for the rest of the winter. Or, ask about Mrs. Thompson's decorating business. Or, there was always the car. School would be a last resort as Alan, Mark, and I covered that from all angles the previous night.

The second half of the evening began better than

the first and I didn't need to resort to my preplanned conversations. Alan suggested pizza when we left the movie, and I must have relaxed because I was talking and laughing normally without thinking about myself. Mark had lost his self-conscious stiffness and Patti wasn't jabbering every second. The night, which had started as an ordeal, had become fun — until we finished eating and were leaving Tony's Pizza Shop. Just as we reached the door, four boys came in. Wes, Danny Brooks, Todd Loring, and Charlie.

Everybody stopped and spoke. I went rigid when Charlie said, "How've you been, Wendy?" managing to come back with "Fine" in a shaky voice, not daring to look into his eyes although he was staring at me. My gaze focused on his left cheek because I had to look somewhere. The squareness of his jaw was the same as always and he was smiling a smile that made my heart jump.

"Did you have a nice Christmas?" he asked.

Before I could reply Danny cut in with, "Listen, fellows, we'd better hurry if we want any food. This place closes in twenty minutes."

They moved toward the counter to order while we walked outside into the parking lot.

The air was freezing and a small gust of wind sent dead leaves and a torn paper cup skittering across our path. Patti started telling about the time her uncle tried to buy pizza in a Chinese restaurant, and I never heard the ending, which must have been hilarious from the way both boys laughed, because my thoughts were on Charlie. *For the rest of my life would I break up inside if I was near him?*

Would my heart always pound when I heard his voice? Did the pain in me show?

Alan stopped at the Simmses' without cutting off the engine, and I said something polite when the others agreed we four should plan another evening together soon. Mark got out with Patti to walk her to the house.

"Patti and Mark seem to click," I murmured just to be speaking.

"They sure do. I never realized she had so much personality or — " He broke the sentence off, looking past me toward Patti's door. "Mark's gone inside with her!" he said. "I can't believe it! I always thought he was Mr. Shy."

I was amazed, too. Had they gone in so they could kiss without Alan and me seeing them? Patti, the reserved girl, and Mark, the shy boy?

Several moments later Alan reached for the ignition switch and turned off the car engine. The radio and heater stopped at the same time.

"I hope you don't mind getting cold," he said in an annoyed tone. "I didn't think it would take my brother so long to say good night to a girl he's practically never spoken to before now, especially when he hasn't had enough nerve to line up a date for himself in his entire life."

"It's good they like one another. You never know about a blind date."

"Are you cold, Wendy? Sorry about the heater, but it wouldn't be smart for us to sit here with the engine off and the heater running. I'm not much in the mood for a case of carbon monoxide poisoning."

I said I wasn't, either. The temperature in the

car dropped quickly and I tried not to shiver. Alan, growing more irked by the second, snapped that if Mark wasn't back in another sixty seconds he was going to drive off and make his brother walk the four miles home.

"At this time of night in such cold weather? Isn't that a trifle drastic?" I tried to put a light note in my voice, and I forced a laugh.

Alan laughed, too, and seemed less tense, but he was immediately serious.

"It shook you up to see Charlie Peterson, didn't it?" he asked.

The question was unexpected, and I swallowed hard. "No. I mean — No . . ." Lying was futile. The evening was already spoiled, and Alan must have guessed the truth or he wouldn't have brought up Charlie's name.

"Yes," I admitted. "I didn't realize it was so obvious."

"Are you still in love with him?"

That time I lied. I couldn't say, *Yes, I'll always love Charlie.*

"Not — not actually in love." My voice wavered. "It's just . . . just that after dating him for such a long time, I guess I'll have to get accustomed to not dating him."

"That figures. I'll bet it's been tough for you, though."

If you only knew . . .

To get the talk away from Charlie and me, I said, "What about you, Alan? Do you date a lot? I guess I was thinking about the girl you brought to the school mixer last fall."

"The girl at the mixer? Oh, you mean Bonita Elliott?"

"The one with the lovely blond hair."

He would think I remembered her. I wished I hadn't asked about the gorgeous blonde, but I wanted very much to know if he felt about her as I did about Charlie. I suppose what I really wanted to find out was if he'd also been pushed aside by someone he loved.

"Bonita is my cousin. Our mothers are sisters," he said. "She and Aunt Grace were visiting us last September. I wasn't sure Bonita would enjoy the mixer since she'd already graduated from high school in Florida where they live, but she acted like she was having a ball."

Mark bounced out of the Simmses' house, smiling so broadly his teeth gleamed during the brief instant he passed beneath the porch light. Alan grunted, "At last!" and started the car. The heater came on with the ignition, first blowing cold, then sending out warm air.

Rather than getting in the back seat, Mark, who had begun to whistle, sat next to me which meant I had to slide over to make room for him. Alan didn't budge.

"Mark, do you think Wendy and I enjoy being icicles?" Alan growled.

"Sorry." Mark sounded too elated to be sorry about anything. "Besides, I wasn't that long."

"The hell you weren't! Over twenty minutes! I timed you after you went in."

"Mark, do you plan to see Patti again?" I interrupted them to try to keep peace.

I was surprised at myself. For more than a month, I'd been on the receiving end of personal questions and furious because of it. Here I was asking an equally personal question of somebody else, of a boy I scarcely knew. My only excuse was that I was anxious to stop the twins from what appeared to be a confrontation.

Mark apparently didn't object. "You bet your buttons!" he exclaimed. "Tomorrow night, for starters. Patti is a great girl, just great."

Without moving my head, I glanced sideways at Alan. The dashboard light showed his lips clamped shut and tiny frown lines were in his forehead. If the next evening was to be a double date, nothing was mentioned about including me.

I wondered if Alan was too mad at Mark to think beyond the present, or if I'd been too boring a date for him to be interested in another evening with me. Maybe my reaction to seeing Charlie killed any idea he had of dating me again. With a jolt I recalled that on Christmas night Alan also mentioned Charlie.

Who could blame Alan? I thought. I knew I'd been a dud, and no boy in his right mind would waste time on a second date with that kind of a girl.

Mark was whistling once more. I didn't recognize the song although it had a happy, lilting melody.

At my house Alan left the motor running when he and I got out, a sure indication he didn't plan to linger with me. Our porch light was burning just as Patti's had been. That was of no concern to him as he hurried me past the cedar tree shadows and waited impatiently on the top step, several feet from me, while I unlocked the door.

There was a catch in my throat as I said, "I had a good time tonight, Alan."

"Yeah. So did I. See you, Wendy."

His dash to the car looked as if he was trying to set a track record.

My stomach muscles knotted. Patti may have received a good-night kiss, but I hadn't and, for some unknown reason, it was a disappointment. Charlie's kisses were what I wanted, I reminded myself. Still, it hurt that Alan had not even held my hand once during the evening.

Angie came over the next morning to see my Christmas gifts, and she scarcely had her coat off before she asked about my date with Alan. I knew she would get to that subject before she left. I hadn't intended going into much detail about the evening, but there was a lot of frustration inside me and I found myself saying things to her I'd meant to keep to myself.

It was cold and overcast, the sort of day that's good to stay indoors. She and I had the house to ourselves as Mom and Dad were at work and Helen was getting a haircut. I poured Coke into two glasses, put some cookies on a plate, and we settled ourselves on the den couch, Angie with her feet tucked under her.

"Last night was fun," I said in reply to her query. That was the identical vague answer I'd made when Mom inquired about the evening with Alan.

"Wes phoned after he came home from bowling."

Angie reached for another cookie. "The phone woke Dad up and you know how annoyed he is when that happens. He would only let me talk a few minutes. Wes said he saw you and Alan at Tony's Pizza Shop and that Mark was there, too. With Patti Simms, of all people! I didn't know those two were dating. In fact," — she sounded faintly accusing — "you didn't tell me you and Alan were doubling, Wendy."

"It didn't seem important."

I wondered silently why people blamed girls for gossip. Boys were just as quick to do it. Wes couldn't wait until morning to report to Angie.

"Did Alan ask you for another date, Wendy?" she said.

"He told me he'd 'see me,' whatever that means." My mouth felt as dry as if it had been dusted with talcum powder. I might have stopped there if I hadn't looked at Angie, but our eyes met and something in me exploded.

"No, he didn't ask for another date and I'm not surprised," I blurted out. "He must have been bored to bits. What's wrong with me, Angie? I've never had trouble getting along with boys and I could talk to Charlie about everything. Just everything! But last night I was positively stupid with Alan. I was uptight and horribly silent, and I'd just begun to relax a little when we left the pizzeria and I came face-to-face with Charlie, which unnerved me all over again."

"Last night was your first date since you and Charlie broke up. Give yourself time. You'll be okay on your next date with Alan."

"He won't call me. I know he won't."

"You look like you're going to cry, Wendy."

"I feel like it."

"If a date with Alan Thompson is that important, you must have gotten over Charlie."

The tightness in my throat grew worse. Angie didn't grasp my situation if she thought I had forgotten Charlie or stopped aching for him. I knew I'd never "get over" Charlie, but I needed to believe other boys liked me a little, that I wasn't the most unattractive girl in the universe, which was how I'd felt the past month.

"If you don't hear from Alan in a couple of days, why don't you phone him? Say you wanted to let him know how much you enjoyed last night."

"I can't." It was a groan.

"Why can't you?"

"I . . . I'd feel . . ." I floundered for the right word. "I'd feel funny. If Alan and I had been dating a while, that would be different. But to call him after I was such a washout last night . . . No way. I couldn't."

Angie jiggled the ice around in her glass. "Would you go out with him if he asked you?"

"He won't."

"You didn't answer my question. Would you date him if he asked you?"

"I guess I would." I gave a small sigh. "If *he* did the asking. Don't hold your breath, though."

"I'll do better than that. I'll invite him — "

"Angie MacLawhorn, don't you dare! If you ask Alan to date me I'll never speak to you again."

"Let me finish. I'm going to have a party New Year's Eve. A real party — not just two or three couples like the last time — and I'll invite Alan and tell him to bring you. You promised to come to my next party — remember?"

"You cooked this up this very second." I sounded as bitter as I felt, already embarrassed about the previous evening without having her force Alan into a repeat.

"I didn't, Wendy. Honest. I was going to tell you about the party before, but I haven't had a chance. Last night Karen and I talked about finding some excitement for New Year's Eve. She said she'd been trying to coax her parents into letting her have a party, but they won't do it. They have an invitation for that night and don't want a bunch of teenagers in the house unless they're around. So, this morning I asked Mom if I could have a party, and she said yes."

Angie looked at me as if she expected me to comment. I was still seething at the thought of her forcing Alan and me together.

"I got the usual antibooze lecture from Mom," Angie went on, her mouth twisting, "about how she and Dad won't serve alcohol to teenagers even if it is New Year's Eve, and that if anyone brings beer, wine, or whiskey, this will be the last party I ever have. I told her she needn't worry. Everybody knows that at my house it's Cokes or fruit punch, but we do provide plenty of food."

"Just don't call Alan," I begged. "He hasn't been at your other parties, and it would put him on the spot now."

"He can always refuse the invitation, Wendy."

I gazed past her through the den window at the bleak winter sky which was a pearl gray color with clouds resembling dark polka dots low on the horizon. My mind was whirling. I had to think of something to convince her not to push Alan and me together.

The boys' car. It hit me like a flash.

My breath came out slowly at the realization that the car was a perfect solution. Mark had driven on Christmas and Alan drove December 26th, which meant Mark would have first say-so about the car on New Year's Eve. I explained that to Angie in a frantic attempt to keep her from including Alan, but it failed.

"I'll invite Mark and Patti, and you four can ride together," she said. "I've always liked Patti."

"New Year's Eve is Helen's last night at home," I mumbled.

"Oh, come off it, Wendy! You know Helen and her boyfriend aren't going to hang around your house New Year's Eve just because she has to go back to school the next day. Besides, you used Helen as an excuse before, and it wasn't very logical then, either."

Apparently nothing would change Angie's mind. Setting my empty glass on a paper napkin on the coffee table, I clasped both hands around my knees.

"It's your party and you can invite the people you want," I said softly. "I'm not asking you *not* to include Alan. But please don't mention anything to him about bringing me."

She must have sensed that I was truly upset because the exasperation went out of her face; when she spoke again, it also was gone from her voice.

"Wendy, if circumstances were different, if you and Charlie were still dating, it wouldn't matter if you came to the party or not. I'd miss you if you didn't show, but, well, I wouldn't worry about it. Now, though, you've been in a cocoon since Thanksgiving and you're just starting to come out of it. That's why you shouldn't backtrack. I want you at this party."

That's how we left it. I didn't promise to come, and she didn't promise to forget about inviting Alan.

chapter
11

The four days between Angie's visit on the twenty-seventh of December and the end of the year crept by in a dreary fashion. I helped Mom in the house, went shopping twice with Helen, and finished a term paper for English. It was a huge contrast to the fun Charlie and I'd had in the past during the time after Christmas until the opening of school.

There was no word from Alan. Nothing.

At first I tried to convince myself I wasn't surprised — I didn't expect to hear from him — but, deep down, I hoped desperately he would ask me out at least once more. When he didn't, the humiliation throbbed in the bottom of my stomach. I decided that he must have invited me to go to the movies to "pay back" for the sandwiches he ate at my house on Christmas night.

It wasn't that I was in love with Alan or thought I ever could be; I didn't want to be seriously involved with him, but I was going through a rough time and needed reassurance. I needed to stop feeling unattractive and unwanted. Too, I wanted friendship with a boy, the sort of friendship Charlie and I enjoyed in addition to loving each other.

If Alan had phoned just to talk, whether he asked me for for a date or not, it would have helped. *First Charlie, now Alan,* I thought. *I'm not pretty enough or cute enough or smart enough or desirable enough to attract and hold a boy.* I was fighting the empty sensation that comes when you realize you aren't wanted.

Helen was another reason those days before the start of the new year seemed different. Stan was out of town on a ski trip and Helen stayed home every night. She was as restless as I was, but not as withdrawn because she knew their separation was temporary and that Stan missed her.

The high spot of her evening came on the dot of nine P.M. when he telephoned long distance. At the first ring she would race upstairs to take the call on the extension for privacy, yelling, "Somebody answer but hang up when you hear me say 'Hello.' " Returning to the den a little later, she was dewy-eyed, her mouth soft from whatever she and Stan said to each other.

One night when Helen rejoined the family after talking to Stan, Mom glanced up from the crewel footstool cover she was embroidering, a long twist of beige yarn dangling from her needle, and smiled.

"Isn't this nice," she said, her eyes taking in Dad, Helen, and me. "All of us together. Just like it used to be years ago."

"Girls, your mother would like to keep you in diapers forever," Dad chuckled.

"Kids grow up, Mom." Helen took the chair she'd left before going upstairs. "Seriously, aren't you glad? You and Dad wouldn't want Wendy and me underfoot every night, the way we were in grade school days. Would you?"

I ducked my head over the book I was pretending to read. When Helen went back to college, my parents would be stuck with having me at home constantly. On school nights it was taken for granted, but on weekends the girls I knew would be dating and there wasn't much chance of a boy calling me.

Every time the phone rang, I jumped. Occasionally there was a call for me. Karen said she was leaving to spend three days with her married sister and would be back New Year's Eve. "You're coming to Angie's party, aren't you, Wendy?" she asked. I gave a weak yes, clutching the phone so tightly my fingers were numb, wondering if it was a lie or if I would actually go. Her doorbell rang, the chimes echoing through the telephone, and to my relief, our conversation was cut short before she could ask about my date for the party. I didn't know how I'd have replied if she had asked.

Angie checked with me every afternoon, either phoning or dropping by. Wes came with her once and he and Helen got into a long discussion about careers and college. I knew Angie wanted to find out if I'd talked with Alan — or with any boy, I suppose — but she and I didn't say much, each of us waiting for the other to mention the party. She didn't tell me whether she'd included the Thompson twins and when I opened my mouth to ask, the words wouldn't come.

Right after breakfast one morning Patti phoned, thanking me half a dozen times for arranging her first date with Mark.

"I've seen him every night and every afternoon since." Her voice purred with happiness. "Yesterday he took me downtown for brunch, and I've invited him to eat at my house at noon today, which is why I'm calling you so early, Wendy. I won't have time to gab later."

"Then I take it Mark doesn't have a job?" I asked, dying to find out if she'd also seen Alan, but unable to make myself phrase the question.

"He does. He has his morning newspaper route, the same route he has had since he was twelve years old. You wouldn't believe how much his customers like him, Wendy. He says they're always generous with money and gifts this time of year. It can't be easy for him to get out of bed at five o'clock in the morning to deliver newspapers, but it does leave him free the rest of the time. He has such a big route he's not only making his own spending money, but he has a savings account. It's a better deal than Alan's job."

"Oh, Alan has a job?" I hoped I sounded casual.

"Since Christmas he's been working at Sherrill's Drug Store, helping with inventory. Didn't you know that, Wendy? I thought you and Alan . . ." The sentence died.

A gigantic weight seemed to be pressing against my ribs. Sherrill's Drug Store was where Charlie worked. For two years he'd had a job there on Saturdays and during summers.

"Wendy, are you still on the line?" Patti spoke louder than usual.

I got myself together enough to reply. Without explaining how things stood between Alan and me, I asked something about Mark and she talked about him another fifteen minutes — telling me what he liked to eat and his favorite TV programs and how he preferred blue shirts to other colors.

I barely heard her, my thoughts on Alan and Charlie. If they were together for hours on end at Sherrill's, no wonder Alan asked point-blank if Charlie and I still dated. No wonder he wanted to know if I was in love with Charlie.

Had the two of them discussed me? The possibility made me cringe. I had a mental picture of them taking a break at work, maybe sitting on crates of merchandise in the drugstore stockroom, with Alan saying, "I dated your former girl friend once. Dullsville"; Charlie coming back with, "Too bad about Wendy Scott. I wasted a lot of time on her"; Alan replying, "Yeah. Nobody can blame you for calling it quits with her."

Perspiration popped out on my face, dampening my forehead. My body was hot, while my hands, feet, and face felt frozen.

Girls talked about boys and it stood to reason boys discussed girls just as much, but I didn't want the only two guys I'd ever dated to be talking about me. For a frantic second I was thankful not to be going with either of them. That sensation evaporated quickly and my desolation returned, the awful lump in my throat hardening at the dismal prospect of being alone, not just New Year's Eve, but maybe forever.

chapter
12

Lunch was almost ready when Mom came in from work at midday on New Year's Eve. Cheese and bacon sandwiches were toasting under the broiler, their rich scent filling the kitchen, and I'd opened a can of tomato soup. My mother ate so little breakfast she was usually ravenous at lunchtime, and while I was too troubled to care about food at the moment, if I didn't eat something she would want to know if I was sick.

"That looks good, dear. Where's Helen?" Mom gestured toward the table set with only two places. "Isn't she having lunch with us?"

"Stan got in early. He came for her about an hour ago. 'Nuff said."

My mother finished washing her hands and reached for the yellow towel hanging by the sink. "That takes care of Helen," she said. "I suppose she'll be home eventually to change clothes before the night's festivities, but we probably won't see much of her otherwise. What about you, Wendy? Are you doing anything tonight?"

Not, *What are you doing tonight?* But, *Are you doing anything?* This was the first time she'd asked me the direct question. She was bound to know I didn't have plans or they already would have been mentioned. I was holding the saucepan, ready to ladle soup into our bowls.

Doing something — doing anything — on New Year's Eve loomed that day as the largest necessity of my life. For the past week I'd worried about it; now, I was in a panic. Among my friends, the final night of the year hadn't seemed special until all of us turned sixteen, but since then, having a date for New Year's Eve was important.

Mom was waiting for my answer. "I . . . I . . ." I began.

The telephone rang.

"I'll get it!" I hurried to the den, relieved to postpone answering my mother if only for a moment. I was breathing hard, and my "Hello" was faint. The voice at the other end of the line was very clear.

"Wendy, how've you been?" Alan Thompson asked.

"Fine." It was the lie of the century, but that wasn't important. "And you, Alan?"

"Never better. I realize I'm late calling you, but I didn't know until a few minutes ago whether or not I'd have to work tonight. I'm just temporary now, although there's a chance for me to get a permanent job here Saturdays, which is why I didn't want to tell the boss I wouldn't stay late tonight at the warehouse if we didn't finish inven —"

"Did you say *warehouse?*" I cut in.

"The warehouse for Sherrill Drug Company. That's where I've been working these last four days and nights. The warehouse is way out on Cranford Road, not downtown near the retail store although it's all one outfit."

I sat down on the nearest chair. Charlie worked at the downtown Sherrill's, which meant the boys probably hadn't been thrown together for hours at a stretch as I'd feared. Maybe they hadn't even seen one another — or had the opportunity to talk about me.

"Wendy, this job is the reason I haven't been in touch with you since the night we went to the movies," Alan continued. "Would you believe every pill and cotton ball on the premises has to be counted for inventory? Medicines, cosmetics — all the stuff Sherrill's sells. I've been working from seven in the morning until ten at night. The boss just announced we're going to finish about six o'clock tonight and — Oh, gosh! I have to scram! This is my lunch break and it's nearly over, which only gives me a couple of minutes to get back to the warehouse to the hair spray and shampoo. That's what I was counting last. 'Bye for now."

The phone clicked as the line went dead, and it rang again at once.

"Wendy, I was yakking about my job and never finished about tonight." Alan spoke so fast his words slurred together. "Will you go to Angie MacLawhorn's party with me?"

Warmth washed over me and my answer came out like music. "I'd love to, Alan."

He rang off the second time. I didn't walk to the kitchen; I floated.

Mom smiled as I sat down opposite her at the table. "From your end of that conversation I gather you were talking to Alan Thompson," she said.

A hopefulness was in her eyes, and I told her Alan was taking me to the party, conscious that there was so much more I wanted to say and couldn't. I wanted her to know I still loved Charlie, but I liked Alan and was happy to hear from him. I wanted her to know how miserable I'd been, as if she couldn't guess, and that if Alan wanted to date me, especially for a party where we'd be with people both of us knew well, I couldn't be as drab and dull as I thought.

Yet, it was impossible to put that into words at the moment. The sentences stuck in my throat. Lifting my head, I looked at Mom. She understood. It was written all over her face and while I watched her, three little frown lines between her eyebrows vanished. She had been worried about my not going to the party and being with my friends, but now she looked relieved. My mother and I didn't always have to talk to communicate.

"Eat your lunch before it gets cold, dear," she said.

I took a small bite of my sandwich. It was delicious, the bacon crunchy with the warm cheese melted against the bread. Wisps of steam rose from the red soup, and the spoon felt cool and smooth to my fingers. Earlier I hadn't been hungry, but all of the sudden I was starving.

* * *

Alan came for me in a different car that night, a tan and brown hardtop that belonged to his parents.

"Wendy, you accomplished a miracle when you fixed Mark up with Patti," he said. "I've never seen my brother like he is now. He has so many stars in his eyes he can scarcely see well enough to squeeze toothpaste on his toothbrush."

"Patti is wild about him, too. She can't talk about much else." Drawing a long breath, I remembered how positive I'd been once that Charlie and I had the most permanent love in the world. "Alan, do you suppose this could be the real thing with Mark and Patti?" *Whatever the real thing is,* I added silently.

"I don't believe Mark could hack anything any realer." He grinned at me. "I'll bet the English teachers at Roosevelt High would disapprove of my saying 'realer.'"

"I'll bet you're right," I came back, laughing.

People passing Angie's couldn't doubt that a party was in progress. Lights glowed in the windows and stereo music sounded out to the street. Cars were bumper to bumper along the curb, which meant we had to park two blocks away; as we walked through the cold to the MacLawhorn house, Alan reached for my hand. Both of us wore gloves so it wasn't a particularly personal touch and I tried not to think about the way Charlie used to take off one of my gloves and one of his when he and I walked together in winter, his palm warm to my fingers.

Mrs. MacLawhorn met us at the door and after I introduced Alan to her, she said, "The party is downstairs. You know the way, Wendy."

Angie and Wes had done a great job of decorating. We smiled at a cardboard sign by the entrance to the recreation room that read: "Enter Only If You Constantly Break Your New Year's Resolutions." Inside, crepe paper streamers in pastel blues, greens, corals, and yellows fanned out from the overhead light fixture to the four walls, giving the ceiling a rainbow effect. Cardboard cutouts of Father Time and the New Year Baby stood on the punch table, and a freshly painted wheelbarrow held bottled drinks packed in crushed ice. Bowls of popcorn and baskets of cheese and crackers were everywhere.

Alan and I must have been among the last guests to arrive as the place was crowded. Three couples were dancing, while most people stood in groups. Angie hurried up to greet us — and at that instant I saw Charlie.

He was on the far side of the room looking down at a girl, and my face muscles tightened. I closed my eyes to steady myself, forcing them open again. I hadn't been searching the room for Charlie — not consciously. At home I'd vowed not to do that, but it was easier to discipline myself in my own bedroom than when Charlie and I were a few feet apart.

He must have sensed that I was looking at him because he glanced at me and waved, promptly turning his attention back to the girl. I didn't know her, but I hated her because she was so beautiful. She was small with glossy black hair and luminous brown eyes which gazed raptly at Charlie, her pale pink dress clinging to a perfect body.

"Wendy, Alan, glad to see you," Angie said. "I guess you know everyone here. Almost everyone.

The only person who doesn't go to Roosevelt is Abby Wilkins, the girl Charlie Peterson brought. She's a senior at Parkview High."

Angie was making that explanation for my benefit. I could sense it. Somebody called to her and she moved away. *Don't think about Charlie, don't think about Charlie,* I repeated to myself, and when Alan said, "Wendy, Mark is motioning to us," I went with him across the room to where Mark and Patti were waiting.

I talked to a lot of people that night, but not to Charlie who was so busy drooling over Abby Wilkins he never left her side. He didn't make a point of introducing her to me, and I was thankful for it. I hadn't been able to answer him coherently at the pizza restaurant, and I would have been even more tongue-tied with his date standing between us.

About ten minutes before midnight Wes gave a screeching whistle to quiet the crowd, and Angie announced that she was turning on the TV so we could watch the celebration at New York City's Times Square and know the exact moment the new year arrived. I found a seat, and Alan perched on the arm of my chair. Angie and Wes passed out noisemakers and paper hats.

Most of the lights in the room were off and the place was dim when the television came on. As the ball began to drop on the screen, all of us joined in the countdown. ". . . seven, six, five, four, three, two—Happy New Year!" and, before I realized what was happening, Alan had one hand cupped under my chin to tilt my face to his, and he kissed me on the mouth.

Maybe I shouldn't have been surprised, but I was. The kiss wasn't passionate and we didn't even hug, but his hand was warm against my chin and his lips were firm on mine. I remembered that everybody kisses at midnight on New Year's Eve and the others at the party were kissing and the television orchestra was playing "Auld Lang Syne" with firecrackers popping outside. My paper hat slipped off, dangling around my neck on its elastic band, and my vision was so blurred it was hard to make out Alan's features, even though he was near enough for me to feel his breath fluttering against my cheek.

"Happy New Year, Wendy," he said softly.

"The same to you."

I was trying to think of a remark to add, something friendly and personal without being sugary, when Mr. MacLawhorn's voice boomed from the doorway. "Food, everybody!" he sang out. "You kids don't want to start the year hungry, do you?" He carried a huge tray of sandwiches, and Mrs. MacLawhorn followed with a sheet cake iced in chocolate.

"Talk about breaking the psychological moment," one of the boys said from a corner of the recreation room. "Who needs food if you've got love?"

Everyone laughed and I joined in. Angie's parents, I decided, had allowed us about two minutes for kissing.

The party ended soon after we ate, and when Alan and I stepped outside snow was falling which put a white crust on the ground and the rooftops. We exclaimed over it as we walked to the car, the big flakes catching on our shoulders and faces.

"Want to plan something together for tomorrow?" he asked.

"Love to. If this weather keeps up, it might have to be a snowball fight."

"How's your pitching arm, Wendy?"

"Terrible," I said and laughed, shivering in the cold. "I expect television will be on all day at my house, what with the parades and football games. If you'd like to come over and watch — "

"I thought you'd never ask me," he grinned. "I'll also take you out to dinner tomorrow night. With the overtime I made working nights at Sherrill's this week, I can afford it. Let me know tomorrow where you'd like to eat."

"Did you get the Saturday job at Sherrill's warehouse?" I asked.

"Sure did. From seven A.M. to six P.M. I start this coming Saturday."

Conversation ended when we reached my house, and as we left the car Alan took my hand, guiding me through a swirl of snowflakes into the cedar tree shadows away from the porch light. My heart was racing. He was going to kiss me again and I wanted him to, wanted desperately to be kissed and held. My arms went around his neck when he pulled me close.

It wasn't like kissing Charlie. I broke the embrace. I didn't feel any of the wild exhilaration Charlie's kisses always brought, and the realization was jolting. Still, it was good to have Alan care enough about me to plan another date. We whispered good-byes, and I was smiling as I let myself into the house.

Mom and Dad had gone to bed. Helen was still out so I left the porch light and a living room lamp on, tiptoeing up the stairs and past my parents' door. After the party noise, I was acutely aware of the silence in my room. *Charlie,* I thought wistfully. At that very minute, was he kissing Abby? Of course he was, I answered my unspoken question. A boy who didn't kiss a girl as lovely-looking as she was would be a fool — and Charlie wasn't stupid.

Don't think about Charlie. Don't think about Charlie, I ordered myself just as I'd done earlier in the evening, knowing it was a futile command with all the yearning tugging at me. As I undressed, I made a decision about the future: I would go out with every boy who asked me because keeping busy was the best means of trying to get my thoughts away from Charlie, if only for a little while at a time.

And if Charlie realized other boys found me fun and liked dating me, maybe, just maybe, he would want me again — if he could tear himself away from beautiful Abby. It didn't hurt to hope.

chapter
13

January always seemed to me the most dismal month of the year. Summer was fun, and in autumn there were crisp, golden days with football games and bright red apples. Thanksgiving and Christmas were wonderful to anticipate. But January — ugh! The weather was apt to be terrible and midterm examinations at the end of the month hung over my head. Spring was centuries off in the distance.

That particular year was no exception. To make things worse, after Charlie left me I'd been too troubled to concentrate on school; a lot of catching up and cramming was necessary in January if my grades were to be decent. I wasn't a straight A student like Patti, but I took pride in bringing home good report cards. Also, if I failed a subject, Mom and Dad would ground me.

The one enjoyable spot was dating Alan on weekends. In spite of our sharing a few kisses, there was nothing serious between us, a fact I felt he realized as much as I did. When proof came, though, it hurt. Perhaps I'd taken Alan too much for granted, or perhaps he wanted to date a girl who turned him on more than I did. I guess the reasons weren't as important as the events.

On the Friday before exam week Alan asked if I'd like to bowl that night. We were leaving the school cafeteria, and he fell into step beside me.

"I'd love it, but I can't tonight," I said. "Today is Dad's birthday and Mom has planned a surprise supper for him at his favorite restaurant downtown. Birthday celebrations are big in our family and I couldn't refuse."

I expected him to ask what I'd like to do Saturday night, but he didn't. We walked down a corridor between rows of gray lockers lining both walls, and Alan stretched out his hand to touch the lockers on his side as we passed. Faint metallic sounds echoed when his fingers tapped the steel doors.

"I'm really in the mood to bowl tonight," he said in an overly casual voice. "If you can't come along, Wendy, I think I'll see if Karen is interested."

My mouth went dry and a strange little prickle inched across the back of my neck. I almost said, "Can't you find a boy to bowl with?" but I caught myself in time, clamping my lips shut.

Karen and Danny Brooks had broken up and she wasn't going steady at the moment. Alan and I weren't, either. After all, I reminded myself somewhat bitterly, Alan had asked *me* first.

I assured myself I wasn't jealous or upset. But I was.

"You and Karen have fun," I said, wondering if I sounded as strange as I felt.

Alan and I did have a date that Saturday night. He phoned from the warehouse during his lunch break Saturday. We went to the movies, doubling with Patti and Mark. Karen's name wasn't mentioned. It took all kinds of willpower not to ask about the bowling.

Days later I discovered I'd benefited indirectly from the bowling episode, because several people from Roosevelt High were at the bowling alley and saw Alan with Karen. Angie told me it now was general knowledge that Alan and I weren't going steady.

Word must have reached Todd Loring since he asked me for a date on the final night of exams. I gave him a quick yes — so quick it made me recall how Patti responded the morning I contacted her about a blind date with Mark Thompson. Everybody celebrated the end of exams and I was glad to have something to do. I'd learned the hard way that staying home alone wasn't exciting when my friends were out having fun.

It wasn't a major event with Todd and me. We drove ten miles to go to a junior college basketball game because his older brother played on one of the teams, and on the way home, stopped for hamburgers. I was pleased when he suggested another date.

"You're back in circulation, Wendy," Angie commented the next day. "Good stuff. I can stop worrying about you now. Todd's a great guy. A little on the quiet side, but I guess that's better than yakking every sec the way Danny Brooks does."

I'd rather be with Charlie. The words were in my heart, not spoken aloud because I couldn't talk about Charlie — not even to Angie — without becoming weepy. It still hurt too much.

Surprisingly, I received two valentines from boys, a red satin box of chocolates from Alan and a heart-shaped jar of peppermints from Todd. Both gifts surprised me. Alan and I had been drifting apart, although we still saw each other occasionally, and I'd had only four dates with Todd.

Dad teased me about the valentines. "Your boyfriends have good taste," he said as he ate a chocolate-covered almond after finishing a peppermint. "Good taste in choosing girls as well as in selecting my favorite candies."

He winked at me and I laughed, taking a seat next to him on the den couch. "Since I'm your daughter, could you be slightly biased about good taste in choosing girls?" I asked.

"You better believe it. I'll admit I'm biased where you and Helen are concerned."

If my father had stopped there, everything would have been lovely, but he added, "I'm very glad you're going with a number of boys rather than just one, Wendy. Not that there's a thing wrong with Charlie. He's a fine youngster. It's simply that going steady is bad while you're in high school. These years are the ones when you should meet a lot of different people."

I sucked my breath in. Dad had given me that speech before, and I didn't want to listen to it again. I was trapped, though.

"When I was your age my father told me I ought to kiss a heap of girls before settling down to one, and he was right," Dad went on. "I didn't meet your mother until I was twenty-three, and by then I'd gone with enough girls to be sure she was the right one for me."

Taking a magazine from the coffee table, I riffled the pages. If I'd replied, my voice would have quivered. It seemed that whenever things were going smoothly, Charlie's name would be mentioned and I'd feel myself crumpling inside like wadded-up tissue paper.

The last week in March I came down with a virus. It wasn't a critical illness, although I'd never felt worse in my life, and the doctor told Mom I wasn't to go back to school until my temperature was normal for forty-eight hours.

I phoned Karen on the first Tuesday night in April, when I was practically well, to ask if she'd pick up homework assignments for me. She dropped them at my house late the next afternoon. It was good to see her. Mom had passed the word earlier that I wasn't to have company as I was contagious, and I hadn't seen anybody but my parents for days, although several friends phoned.

Wednesday was blustery and it was hard to realize the calendar now said April. A blast of cold wind came in as Karen opened our front door.

"You're awfully pale, Wendy," she said. "Are you sure you're over it? I don't want to catch whatever you've had."

"Do you think I'd ask you to come here if I was still contagious? Dr. Blanchard says I can go to school tomorrow and I'm looking forward to it. I feel like I've been in jail, cooped up here. What's happening at Roosevelt?"

"Let's see . . . not much, really. Suzanne Howard has cut her hair short, and I do mean short. Oh, there's a new guy in school — Derek Hollis. And is he ever dreamy-looking! He's so handsome I can't stop staring at him."

"Has he asked you for a date yet?" I teased. Karen never had trouble getting dates. She was not only beautiful, but she seemed to exude the kind of charm boys liked.

"Derek hinted, but in case you haven't heard, Danny and I are going steady again." Her cheeks looked very pink and when she said Danny's name, there was a shiny glow in her eyes.

If she and Danny Brooks could break up and get back together, Charlie and I might, too. My heart began to pound.

"Wendy, did you hear what I just asked you?" Karen's voice sliced into my thoughts. I had no idea how long I'd been daydreaming.

"Sure," I fibbed, not sure at all. "About Danny — "

"I asked if you've heard from Charlie. I thought, since you were sick, he would . . ." She waited, looking at me expectantly.

"No, I haven't."

"Maybe you'll like this new guy. If it weren't for the way I feel about Danny, I would. I don't know much about him except that he moved here from Denver and he ought to be in the movies or on TV or modeling for magazine ads, with his looks. You should see his car, Wendy. It's bright red, one of those European sports models. I can never remember the names of foreign automobiles, but this one is long and low to the ground and it purrs."

"Danny had better put you on a leash," I told her and laughed. "If he turns his back, you'll probably be riding around in a certain red car."

"I don't think so. Danny and I have something special this time." She glanced at her watch and jumped up. "I didn't realize it was almost five and I have to run. Danny is coming over tonight and I want to get my homework out of the way before dinner."

"Are your folks letting you date on a school night?" Her parents were as strict about that as mine.

"They won't allow me to go out on a school night, but Mom relented enough to say that occasionally I can have a date at home — if he doesn't stay late. So," she gave a wide smile, "Danny is coming over early."

I stood at the living room window and watched her hurry down Hawthorne Street, the wind lifting her long hair off her shoulders. My mind spun. *If she and Danny . . . then maybe Charlie and I . . .*

chapter
14

When I reached school the next morning a loose-leaf notebook, two textbooks, and a boy's yellow cashmere sweater were piled on my homeroom seat, and I was opening the top book to find out the owner's name when a voice behind me said, "That's my gear."

"But it's my chair," I answered.

Turning around, I was face to face with the handsomest boy I'd ever seen. He had black curly hair and very pale blue eyes, his broad shoulders tapered to a slim waist, and he was so tall I had to look up at him.

"Are you Wendy, by any chance?" he asked.

"Why do you want to know?"

"I'm new here and Mrs. Slocumb told me to 'use Wendy's seat until she comes back.' I've been sitting in this chair for four days and if you're Wendy" — he paused, smiling — "I guess I'll drape myself on a coat hanger and perch on the wall."

It was impossible not to laugh at his crazy remark.

"I'm Derek Hollis," he said.

"And I'm Wendy Scott. You'd think, considering how long Mrs. Slocumb has been teaching school, that she'd have remembered to order a chair for you. I certainly hope she doesn't just call the roll every day and then tell you to take the seat of anybody who happens to be absent."

"I hope so, too. It would be like playing a perpetual game of musical chairs. Where have you been, Wendy? Off on a vacation?"

"Hardly. I was at home, sick with the flu. But I'm all right now."

"You sure are," he came back. I was glad I'd worn an especially becoming outfit, my beige skirt with a brown blouse, instead of jeans. Somehow, the skirt seemed more sophisticated, and I had an idea Derek with his smooth manners and fantastic looks would like sophisticated girls.

Mrs. Slocumb came in and when I handed her the note Mom had written explaining my absence, I mentioned in an undertone that Derek Hollis needed a chair.

"Oh, yes, thank you, Wendy," she answered as if she'd forgotten him. She truly was absentminded.

Derek, his books under one arm and the yellow sweater tossed around his shoulders with the two sleeves looped on his chest, leaned against the rear wall. I took the long route to my seat in order to pass him.

"I reminded her," I whispered, and he gave me one of his beautiful smiles. His teeth were as perfect as the rest of his features.

Derek was in two of my classes and while I didn't have a chance that day to talk to him again at school, it was impossible not to think about him. I found myself sneaking glances in his direction. The other girls in those two classes were eyeing him, too, but, if he realized it, he didn't give any indication. With his looks he's probably conceited and no wonder, I told myself. I found that trying to put him out of my mind was impossible which was why I was flabbergasted at what happened during the afternoon.

After school that Thursday, I was walking home when a red sports car, the engine humming, zoomed up beside me and braked.

"Guess what, Wendy?" Derek leaned his head out of the automobile window. "Slocumb finally got me a chair, and I don't believe she'd have done it if you hadn't prodded her. That means I owe you. Can I pay off the debt with a hamburger?"

"Why . . . uh . . . sure." Surprise showed in my voice.

Derek reached across the car seat to open the door on the passenger side.

"You mean — right now?" I asked, unable to realize this was to be an instant date.

"Why not? Aren't you hungry when you get out of school? I am."

Usually I felt that way, but the intentness of Derek's blue eyes killed any desire I might have had for food. I got into the car with him, feeling as if I was soaring in the stratosphere instead of riding on pavement.

"This is a beautiful car, Derek," I said, just to be saying something.

"Sure is. That's why you look so good in it, Wendy. A beautiful car ought to rate a beautiful girl passenger."

It was corny and he said it in a flippant manner. I should have ignored it or laughed, but I did neither.

"How many times have you made that trite crack to a girl?" I blurted out, surprised at my words.

Derek's remark about the beautiful car rating a beautiful girl passenger didn't mean anything, and maybe it wouldn't have sounded trite to me if I'd actually been beautiful like Karen or Abby Wilkins. I didn't fall into that category, though. I knew I was nice-looking, but not beautiful; Derek's glib beautiful girl bit made me self-conscious.

I was filled with embarrassment. The entire day I'd thought how wonderful it would be to date a boy as handsome as Derek, and now when I had the chance, I'd probably muffed it.

But, rather than getting angry, Derek laughed. "I like girls who say what they think. Okay, I'll confess. I've made that remark before when a girl admired my wheels." He swerved the red car into the parking lot of a drive-in restaurant. "What'll you have with your burger? A shake or a Coke or what?"

He had kept the moment from being awkward, and I leaned limply against the back of the car seat. We began to talk in a casual fashion. Derek asked questions about school, and I found out a little about him. He and his father lived in Brinkley Towers, a new high-rise apartment building, and his father worked for a nationally known firm of stockbrokers that was opening an office in town. I didn't know much about stocks or the people who sold them, but I'd seen that company's ads on television.

"Dad is the person sent in to get the new branch started," Derek explained. "He's good at it, too. That's why he's moved so often. He stays in one area a year or two and then is sent somewhere else."

"Just you and your father?" I asked. "Is your mother dead?"

"They're divorced. Mom lives in Chicago. That's where Dad and I lived, too, until Dad was transferred to the company headquarters in New York and started working with the new branches."

Derek glanced at me and shrugged. "It's no big deal, Wendy," he said. "People get divorced all the time. My mother is a lawyer, and she'd just gotten her practice established in Chicago and didn't want to move. That was eight years ago. When they got the divorce, I mean. I was nine. We see each other."

Talking about his parents' divorce made him tense, in spite of the comment about it not being what he termed "a big deal." To get our conversation on a different track, I asked about the school he went to last. It was in Denver, he said; before that, he and his father were in Santa Fe after leaving New York.

The idea of living so many different places boggled my mind. I couldn't conceive of home being anywhere except Virginia.

The sun had slipped from view, and while it wasn't dark, the air was cooler with the approach of night. I told Derek I should be leaving and gave him directions to my house.

"I was counting on stretching this outing into dinner," he answered without starting the car.

"Thanks, but I do have to go home now."

"Because you already have a date for tonight, Wendy?"

"It isn't that. My mother will be expecting me. In fact, she's probably having a fit right now because I didn't come in after school." I wished instantly I hadn't been so honest. What I said was true, but it sounded infantile when I put it into words.

"Okay," he said. "I'll drive you home to make peace with her, and then we'll decide what we want to do for fun tonight."

"But I can't go out! Not on a school night!"

The white neon sign at the drive-in came on and a brilliant glow engulfed us. Derek's forehead wrinkled and in the blazing artificial light his eyes were filled with disbelief. They seemed more green than blue and they bore into me.

"What are you talking about?" he demanded. "What does a school night have to do with it?"

"I . . . uh . . . there's homework."

"If you have a lot of work, we won't stay out late. We'll just ride around and see if we can locate some action."

"You don't understand, Derek! I can't. My parents don't permit me to date on school nights."

His jaw muscles tensed. "If you don't want to date *me*, just say it!" he snapped angrily. "I'll get the message. You don't have to make up excuses."

"I do want to date you, Derek! Believe me, I do! This rule of my parents about school nights isn't my idea." My voice broke. Derek wouldn't have anything to do with me in the future, and who could blame him? In Denver and New York and Santa Fe, he'd no doubt known girls who didn't have to exist by their parents' Victorian regulations.

There was silence in the red car. He drummed his fingers noiselessly on the dashboard.

"Just what nights are you permitted to date, Wendy?" He accented "permitted."

"Fridays, Saturdays, and Sundays."

"Isn't Sunday a school night?" The sarcasm was unmistakable.

"Yes, but I do my weekend homework early. Before Sunday night. Derek, being with you this afternoon has been great, but I really must go home."

He flipped the ignition switch and backed out of the parking place. I was trying desperately to think of something to say to convince him I wanted to see him again. I wondered if Mom would give me a "No" if I phoned her and announced that I'd be in later. Yes, she would, I decided, choking back a sigh as I vetoed the idea of calling her from the drive-in. She'd ask a million questions about where I was and whom I was with, and it would be a new humiliation to phone her and then have to tell Derek I'd been ordered home.

Half the girls at Roosevelt High would have given anything to be in the red car with Derek Hollis, and I was there and was turning him off fast. The realization made me miserable, and the irony was that for a short time he'd made me feel alive. No boy except Charlie ever sent my pulse racing so furiously.

We reached my block on Hawthorne Street, and I pointed out the house.

"The one with the big cedar in the yard," I said.

"Wendy, did I get this right? When you date, it has to be weekends or afternoons?"

I nodded miserably.

He stopped the car in front of my house, and that's when the miracle happened. Smiling one of his heavenly smiles, he said, "What about tomorrow night? It's a Friday."

I couldn't take it in for a second. "Oh, I'd love it! I really would!"

"Want to know something, Wendy Scott? You're a challenge to me."

"A challenge? Why?"

My hand was on the door handle, but rather than getting out of the car, I waited. In the dusky twilight he looked squarely into my eyes.

"I don't like a girl to turn me down," he said. "And you did. That makes you a first for me. I've never tried to date a girl who operated under such crazy rules."

"They aren't my rules, Derek. I don't like them, but I'm stuck with them, and some of the other girls have the same regulations about dating. I'm looking forward to tomorrow night, though. Thanks for the hamburger."

"Hey — hold it! Don't get out yet. I want a good-bye kiss."

At first I was too stunned to move or speak, and then every nerve in my body came alive. Part of me was dumbfounded at the idea of being kissed in a car parked in front of my house with enough daylight for the neighbors — and Mom — to see us if they were near windows; the other part of me was saying silently, *Don't just talk about it! Do it!*

"Is this another rule, Wendy?" he asked. "No kissing on Thursdays?"

I managed to collect my senses enough to reply. "No, I . . . I . . . Maybe some other time," and I stepped from the car to the sidewalk. My cheeks had to be blood red.

"So you don't do any kissing on a first date, huh?" he grinned. "Like I told you, you're a challenge. You just keep in mind that tomorrow night will be our second date, since today was the first."

After he drove off, I must have stood there three or four minutes, fighting to get myself back to normal before going in the house to face Mom. I was breathing as hard as if I'd been running. If my mother asked where I'd been since school closed — and she would ask — I'd say truthfully that a new boy invited me for a burger. But I didn't want to appear as flustered as I felt.

chapter
15

Dating Derek was different from going out with the other boys I knew. I learned that during the first weekend. We went to a disco Friday night — a place too expensive for the high school crowd — and on Saturday night he took me to a downtown restaurant which had fantastic food and live music. Both evenings ended with sweet kisses in his car after he drove me home, and in the darkness I didn't worry about the neighbors or my parents seeing us. Derek took pains to park away from the street light.

Thinking about those kisses after I was in my room, I was stunned at the intensity of my response to Derek. I wasn't in love with him, but I realized I was attracted by his looks and his sophistication. He was the first boy since Charlie that I liked to kiss.

Was I beginning to "get over" Charlie? I honestly didn't know. I still loved him and deep down in my heart, I still hoped he would want me again, but the first devastating pain at his rejection had become a steady ache that I'd learned to live with. Being with Derek was exciting, and it was great to feel alive again.

Sunday was a gorgeous day, unusually balmy for April — even in Virginia — with the sunshine bright and the air soft. Derek came over in the middle of the afternoon and when he asked what I'd like to do, I suggested that we go to a public park about eight miles out of town. It was part of an estate willed to the county, and it had woods and winding footpaths, along with fountains and large lawns bordered by flowers.

The day was too nice to be indoors and besides, I'd already discovered Derek didn't like the things my other friends enjoyed. He refused to play games like Monopoly or Scrabble, and if he and I were talking, he preferred us to be in his car rather than my house. He was completely disinterested in a double date.

"Who needs that, Wendy?" he'd said when I mentioned going out with Angie and Wes or with Karen and Danny. "Doubling is kid stuff. I asked *you* for a date because I want to be with *you*."

It was flattering to me for him to feel like that and, thinking about it, I decided moving so often kept him from making long-term friendships. He probably was used to knowing people on a one-to-one basis, rather than running around with a group.

We rode out to the park Sunday afternoon to discover lots of other people had the same idea. The grounds were packed. Angie and Wes were leaving as we arrived and the four of us chatted briefly near the entrance, Angie giving me such quizzical glances I knew she couldn't wait to call me and find out about my weekend.

Derek and I had been in the park about an hour when I thought I saw Charlie in the distance. But that particular boy had his back toward me and was half-hidden by the water from one of the big fountains, so I couldn't be positive. I didn't know if Derek had heard anything about Charlie and me, and I dreaded having him ask about it, so I ignored the boy who might have been Charlie. It was too pleasant a day to discuss something hurtful.

At sunset the crowd in the park thinned out. We found seats on a wooden bench by a bed of lavender hyacinths that were just beginning to open, the flowers giving off a heady fragrance. Blooms on some nearby Japanese quince bushes made dabs of coral against the green lushness of the grass.

"Beautiful, isn't it?" I said softly. "I love spring."

"Right now I think some food would be just as beautiful. Where would you like to eat tonight, Wendy?"

I turned sideways on the bench to face him. "You've spent plenty on me these past few days. Why don't we go to my house and make sandwiches or have bacon and eggs?"

"Will your folks be there?"

"Yes, but — "

He wouldn't let me finish. He was already shaking his head. "No way, Wendy. We wouldn't have any privacy."

That made no sense. Why would we need privacy to eat? I thought the question without asking it. Derek had seemed ill at ease when I introduced him to my parents Friday night, and since then, he'd scarcely said a word to them except hello when he came to the house for me. Both Mom and Dad attempted to draw him into conversation, and he'd been polite but not responsive.

"My parents won't hover over us," I went on. "They're good about not doing that, and on Sunday nights they usually eat in the den so they can watch their favorite TV programs. You and I will have the kitchen to ourselves."

I waited for him to answer, and when he didn't, I said, "You don't have a job, Derek, and I can't see your taking me out to eat again tonight."

He leaned down to pick a wide blade of grass, carefully dividing the center into two strips with his thumbnail. "Don't worry about what I spend," he muttered.

"I don't want to bankrupt you and I know how expensive the disco was. That goes double for the restaurant where we ate last night."

It took him a long minute to say anything else. "Maybe I'll get a job when summer comes," he said finally. "But right now, money's not a problem. Dad pays my allowance and Mom sends me plenty on the side." He gave a choppy, mirthless laugh. "Conscience money for both of them, I guess." He tossed the strips of grass to the ground and stood up. "Anyhow, it's swell to have the cash, and you don't hear me griping about spending it on you. I happen to think you're worth it."

The compliment made my mouth curve into an easy smile. "You decide where we'll eat tonight," I told him.

"What about the drive-in where we went Thursday afternoon?"

"Fine. There's a pay phone by the park entrance, and I can call Mom to let her know I won't be there for supper."

It was the wrong thing for me to say. Derek's jaws stiffened. He didn't have to notify anyone about his plans, and he couldn't understand why I needed to tell Mom mine.

"Is that so she can order you to come in early because you have to go to school tomorrow?" His lip curled ever so slightly.

I ignored the remark. "On Sunday nights I do have to get home earlier than on Fridays and Saturdays, Derek."

"Just how early is that?"

"Ten o'clock."

"Ten o'clock is for grade school kids!" he exploded. "Don't you think you're a little old to have to check with your mother every two minutes? Does she tell you when to brush your teeth? Do you have to ask her permission to go to the bathroom?"

The ugliness of his tone shocked me. Derek must have realized how he sounded because his face reddened, and he said, "Sorry, Wendy. I didn't mean to come on so strong."

He was embarrassed and I felt sorry for him. I began to chatter, saying anything impersonal I could think of to give him a chance to unwind. I mentioned the eccentric bachelor brothers who, although they never permitted a soul to set foot on their land, willed their estate to the county for a public park. Pausing, I waited for Derek to speak and, when he didn't, I kept talking, going into detail about our winning football team the previous autumn and relating classroom incidents that happened before he moved to Virginia. When I got around to Todd Loring putting a live frog in Mrs. Slocumb's top desk drawer three consecutive mornings, Derek chuckled; the laughter apparently got rid of the last of his irritation.

"Did she ever find out who did it?" he asked.

"Not that I heard. But she did lock her desk after the third day and besides, by then Todd was probably getting low on frogs."

Derek and I were at peace again. I felt as though a weight had been lifted off me because I couldn't bear the idea of anything coming between us.

On the ride from the park into town I mulled all of it over. He didn't have brothers or sisters and he'd had little personal contact with his mother. There had never been a hint that he was especially close to his father. How could he be expected to know first-hand about close family relationships?

Along with discovering that Derek didn't want to double-date, I'd learned there were some topics guaranteed to annoy him and best left unmentioned. Rules and regulations, for one. Questioning his decisions once he'd made up his mind what he wanted, for another. Anything about parents — his, mine, or someone else's. When I dated other boys, I hadn't consciously needed to avoid certain subjects the way I did with him, but then, "other boys" weren't as exciting as Derek Hollis.

The half-moon was a pale, creamy color and stars peppered the black sky when we left the drive-in shortly after eight. Derek steered the red car with one hand, his other arm around my shoulders, and it felt wonderful there. I was relaxed, happier than I'd been in a long time, and it never occurred to me those feelings would vanish in less than an hour.

"Where are we going?" I asked as he turned the car in the opposite direction from my house.

"Back to the park. Let's see how it looks in the moonlight."

"The park is closed now, Derek. The gates are locked at seven this time of year. Later in the summer, when the afternoons are longer, they'll stay open until eight."

"I know that. I saw the sign at the entrance." He winked at me. "So much the better for us. It ought to be a great spot for privacy."

"You won't find any privacy there. Guards with dogs patrol inside and outside the gates. The police have broken up some drug parties in the area; two years ago a couple in a car got mugged at night, and the girl died from injuries. After that, county authorities had the lights installed and hired security guards."

"Wellll" — he drew the word out — "I'm glad you warned me. You've lived here all your life. You must know places where we *can* have privacy."

"You're obsessed with that word 'privacy.' " I laughed.

"I don't dig doing my loving in public."

I suggested that we go to my house, and promptly wished I hadn't mentioned it. I should have known better after our earlier conversation. Derek became rigid, his arm instantly heavy across my shoulder. I didn't want another bad scene, especially when everything was so right.

"My idea of privacy isn't kissing you with your family in the next room," he muttered.

"We don't have to go *into* my house, Derek. The street was private enough for us Friday and Saturday nights."

I expected him to agree, but he didn't. Ever since I'd described the situation at the park, he'd been driving aimlessly, and we were in a rather shabby residential district. Lights burned in most of the dilapidated houses, although two dwellings were dark. Both had unkept yards and overgrown shrubs that almost hid their FOR SALE signs. Derek's car was the only one moving on the block, and I didn't see anyone walking.

He stopped in the middle of the street and shifted into reverse gear, backing into the driveway between the two empty houses, the scraggly bushes swishing against the sides of the car.

"What are yo — " I began, but never finished the question. In one swift motion he cut off the engine and car lights and swooped me into his arms.

I leaned against him, losing myself in his embrace, until I realized we were caught up in something stronger than what I wanted. "No, Derek," I whispered and put my palms on his chest, shoving him back.

"Don't you want me to love you?" he asked angrily.

"I do. You know I do. I want you to kiss me. But not anything else."

He reached out for me again — ignoring what

I'd just told him — his mouth urgent and fiery against mine.

"Derek, *no!*" I gasped. He was holding me so tightly it took all my strength to twist away. My back was pressed against the car door on the passenger side, the arm rest biting into my spine.

"You're the damnedest girl I've ever seen!" he blurted out. "You led me on and quit!"

"I didn't lead you on. I mean — if I did, it wasn't intentional. I think we'd better leave here, Derek. Let's go now."

He didn't touch the ignition switch.

"What's the matter with you?" he growled. "You act like we're living a hundred years ago. This is the twentieth century — or haven't you heard?"

My throat muscles tightened, and it took a lot of willpower for me to keep my voice steady. "I do know it's the twentieth century," I measured each word out. "And I have feelings, too. I love kissing you and I love having your arms around me, but it has to stop at that."

"You're unreal."

"A lot of girls feel the way I do."

"Quit kidding yourself. I'll tell you one thing, Wendy. If you won't, there are plenty of girls who will!"

If he was trying to hurt me with that last comment, he succeeded. But he also made me mad. Something clicked deep in my brain, and I recoiled as if I'd been slapped. Until that instant, no boy had ever threatened me, and that's what Derek was doing.

I sat up very tall, rigid with anger. "If you feel

like that" — I emphasized each word — "you're probably wasting your time with me. I think we should say good-bye right now so you can find a girl who suits you more than I do."

His answer was to start the motor and barrel out of the driveway into the street. I caught my breath. Neither of us spoke. A giant hand seemed to be squeezing my chest, making it hard for me to draw enough oxygen into my lungs, and I was terrified I'd burst into tears in front of him. Anger and hurt and frustration were all tangled up in me, and I didn't want to give him the satisfaction of watching me cry.

At my house Derek hit the brakes so hard my neck jerked forward. I wanted to say something and didn't know how to put my thoughts into words since apparently he hadn't grasped what I told him earlier. Still, I wanted to try.

"I wish we hadn't had this disagreement," I began. "We've had a lot of fun until tonight and . . ."

The sentence trailed off. He gave no indication that he heard me. Gunning the engine, he stared straight ahead. I opened the car door, almost falling as I got out. In his rush to be away from me he accelerated quickly, his tires screeching against the pavement.

Our living room drapes were open and I could see Mom seated at the desk. Apparently she was writing a letter and she must have heard Derek's tires because she lifted her head and at the same time, raised her pen from the paper. Then she resumed writing. There was an air of calmness and peace about her but instead of soothing me, the sight added to my turmoil. It wasn't fair for me to be so distraught and for her to be so serene.

I dreaded going in. She would ask why I was home thirty minutes early, which was unheard of. If she had a good look at my face, she'd realize I was upset and I couldn't tell anyone what happened. Maybe eventually I would want to talk about it, but not yet.

Still, I couldn't stand on the dark street indefinitely by myself. The tears I'd been holding back were trickling slowly down my cheeks, and I stumbled toward the cedar tree in our yard, shrinking into its black shadow. The kissing spot, that's what Charlie used to call that special place. The huge, familiar lump surged into my throat at the memory of how Charlie and I would stand in the cedar shadow and kiss. I'd had love and security then. Charlie had never threatened me. I'd lost Charlie, though. Now, I'd also lost Derek.

Maybe Derek was right and I was wrong, I thought ruefully. Maybe my set of values was too old-fashioned for the present.

But I knew it was right for me.

chapter
16

Angie was waiting at my locker when I reached school Monday morning, and just as I anticipated, she was full of questions.

"Tell me about Derek Hollis!" Her voice bubbled with excitement. "He's the best-looking guy I've ever seen! Of course, Wes is great-looking, too, and he's the one I love, but Derek is fantastically handsome. How many dates did you have with him over the weekend? Where did he take you? When will you see him again? Wendy, are you going steady with him?"

I would have told Angie the truth if Karen hadn't joined us before I could answer.

"Wendy, you've been holding out on me!" Karen was one big smile. "You and Derek — and all of it happening in such a hurry! Do you realize it's been less than a week since I delivered those homework assignments to you and told you he'd moved to town? Instant romance. That's one for the record books."

"We've had a few dates. That's all." I prayed my voice sounded casual. "It probably won't replace King Edward VIII and Mrs. Simpson in history."

"How is it to kiss Derek?" Karen asked slyly.

I must have blushed. My cheeks felt rosier than normal. I should have stated bluntly that Derek and I were finished, but I couldn't spell it out. Pride probably had something to do with my hesitancy. It was humiliating to admit not being able to hold a boy for longer than a weekend.

"You gals should get the stardust out of your eyes," I came back and forced a laugh. "Derek just moved here and he doesn't know many people. He took me out to eat and we had fun, but that's all there is to it. Maybe we'll date again and maybe we won't."

"Wendy" — Angie put one hand on my arm — "don't compare him with Charlie. Just accept Derek and enjoy being with him. When Wes and I saw you and Derek at the park yesterday you were positively radiant, and I hope this means a new era for you."

I wasn't radiant Monday morning. Far from it. I hadn't slept much and there were gray circles around my eyes. Every nerve in my body was stretched taut.

The first bell sounded and since neither Karen nor Angie was in my homeroom, we went off in different directions. I exhaled slowly with relief at not having to continue gabbing with them about the weekend.

A fresh ordeal lay ahead of me, though. Facing Derek. I'd been steeling myself for it ever since waking up that morning.

Sunday night after I stopped crying and got myself together enough to leave the cedar shadows and go into the house, Mom was on the phone talking to her boss at the crafts shop and Dad was deep in a murder mystery. Poking my head in the den door, I said good night to them and hurried upstairs, thankful not to have to linger. If Mom had asked where Derek and I went and if I had a good time, I didn't trust myself to give noncommittal answers.

As I walked into Mrs. Slocumb's room Monday, Derek, already in his seat, had his math book open and was writing in his loose-leaf notebook. I had to pass him as he was in the front row near the door, and he didn't raise his head.

I certainly didn't peer at him, but once I was settled in my chair on the far side of the room, I sneaked a glance in his direction. He appeared to be concentrating and I found myself wondering if he was in a rush to complete an assignment, or if he was pretending to study to avoid eye contact with me.

It was like that the rest of the day. He didn't go to the cafeteria at noon, or if he did, it wasn't while I was there; in the two classes we had together he kept his attention focused on the teachers and the blackboard. After a while it dawned on me how much I was watching him, and I made myself stop.

In one sense I was glad he ignored me as we had nothing left to say to each other. But I was hurt. Derek Hollis was the first boy I'd dated who managed to push Charlie from my thoughts, and I was happy with him — until he put an ugly wedge between us.

That Monday afternoon I carried my coat into my last class, so it would be possible to leave school in a hurry when the bell rang. If I had to go to my locker, which was in the same hall as Derek's locker, I might bump into him. It seemed much smarter to dash from the building and have a head start on everyone else.

Small, fluffy clouds drifted across the blue-and-white April sky, the sun alternating with showers. It was what Helen would have described as "an iffy day." I wished my sister were in town. I could have talked to Helen about Derek, but her spring vacation came the end of March and there was little chance she would be home for a weekend soon.

Cradling my books, I walked swiftly, my head down to watch for puddles. I was trying to decide how to explain to Mom why Derek and I were no longer seeing one another after such a flurry of weekend dates, and then I began to wonder why dating was so vitally important. It colored everything in my life and the lives of my friends.

I walked two additional blocks before coming up with a satisfactory explanation. Now that the boys and girls I knew were teenagers, dating took the place of the comradeship we'd shared when we were younger: climbing trees together and playing hopscotch and tag together and spending Saturday mornings watching TV cartoons together. Dating was our way of life, and if it led to going with one special person it was a bonus. I didn't believe I was boy-crazy. I enjoyed being with girls. But it was fun to be involved with a boy, and I didn't want to be dateless any more than I wanted to be without girl friends.

Those thoughts were churning in my brain when an automobile came up beside me. I turned my head to see Derek in his red car, a strange half-smile tugging at his lips.

"Is it safe to speak to you, Wendy?" he asked. "Or do I get a blast of dynamite just for saying hello?"

My heart pounded against my ribs. His voice sounded teasing and serious at the same time.

"I don't know a thing about dynamite," I came back, and both of us smiled. I continued to walk, and the red car rolled very slowly beside me.

"Are you over your mad, Wendy?"

"I wasn't mad. You were the angry one," I added.

"I'm not angry now. Not with you. I ought to have my head examined for messing up our evening." He leaned across the car seat to open the door on the passenger side. "Please get in, Wendy. It's rough to try to talk with you out there and me in here."

I hesitated. Another bitter scene was more than I could endure, even though I wanted to be with him. Derek must have read my mind because he said, "If you're waiting for an apology, I have a million of them. I'd like us to keep dating."

"On my terms?"

"Sure, you Puritan," he grinned. "On your terms if that's the way it has to be. I go for you, Wendy. And I wish I didn't."

"That's not a very flattering statement."

"There I go again, making you mad. I didn't mean it to be a slam."

He appeared genuinely upset and I didn't ask him to explain. I got into the car and his frown instantly changed into a smile.

"Wendy, we need to get this straightened out once and for all," he said. "You and I hit it off on almost everything, and I want to go on seeing you."

"I'd like that — if it's on my terms."

"I thought we'd just covered that."

Smiling, I inched a little nearer him on the car seat. He reached for my hand, covering it with his and squeezing my fingers gently as he turned off Hawthorne Street, left the residential section, skirted several offices, and went past the city limits sign before stopping at an abandoned service station. The cinderblock building was boarded up and the gas pumps were gone. Tall weeds grew through cracks in the cement apron. It was a hideous spot, drab and run-down, although none of that mattered. I didn't see anything but Derek's face when he stopped the car and put both of his arms around me, covering my lips with his.

chapter 17

After Derek and I made up I felt ten feet tall.
The hours rushed along that week. Everything was
so lovely and vibrant that I was overwhelmed by
the colors and scents of spring. I found myself humming when I dressed or did chores, and when I was
outside I had a wild urge to skip rather than walk.

At school Derek and I exchanged soft, lingering
looks, and sometimes he held my hand as we went
down a corridor. Everybody knew we'd discovered
each other.

My mother must have sensed the change in me.
Wednesday night when she and I were doing the
dinner dishes, she asked in a studiedly casual voice
if I was "becoming serious" about Derek.

I made myself busy rinsing coffee cups, averting
my face. "Well, sort of serious . . . I guess," I
mumbled. Then I added, "Not really, though."

She gave me a long look.

"That was a dumb comment I just made, wasn't it?" I laughed nervously. "The truth is that I like Derek a lot. He's the only boy I've dated since Charlie that I'm truly attracted to in more than a friendly way, but — Oh, I don't know how to say it, Mom. I do like him, but I don't feel about him the way I do — did — about Charlie."

Do was the correct word. But I didn't want my mother to know how much I still loved Charlie.

"Wendy, you don't have to be in love with a boy to care about him," she said. "The feeling between you and Charlie was unusually strong, and you may not care that deeply about anybody else until you find the person you want to marry."

But I want to feel that deeply again . . . and be loved in return.

Mom seemed to understand. "He seems like a very nice boy, but your daddy and I don't know him at all," she went on. "Why don't you bring him here more often? Invite him to dinner. Just give me a little notice if he's to eat with us, though."

"Thanks, Mom. I'll do that."

I didn't tell her I'd attempted to bring him to dinner that evening. We were having pot roast, so I knew food wouldn't be a problem, but Derek refused without offering any reason, and I didn't insist when he dropped me at my house after we left the drive-in. He invariably tensed up at the prospect of being in a family group, and everything had been too wonderful since Monday afternoon to risk trouble.

At school Thursday, Angie told me she was having a party on Friday night.

"I haven't had a party since New Year's Eve, and this won't be a biggie like that one," she said. "Just five or six couples tomorrow night, and I want you and Derek to come."

"Sounds lovely to me." I took a long breath. "Angie, you invite Derek."

"Why? I'm inviting you and you can bring any guy you choose. I just said Derek because you're dating him. Usually I only tell half of a couple."

I decided to be honest with her. "You might have to talk him into coming," I said. "It isn't that he's antisocial. But he and his father have moved so much, I don't think he feels at ease in a crowd where everybody else is acquainted."

"Haven't the kids at school been friendly toward him, Wendy?"

"Of course they have. This is just a feeling he has. All of us have our quirks, you know."

"Okay, I'll ask him. Do you realize you're the only person at Roosevelt High who knows Derek Hollis? Really knows him, I mean. Everybody knows his name and where he moved from, but he sure hasn't mingled much."

"He hasn't lived here long," I answered defensively.

Just as I feared, Derek was less than lukewarm about Angie's party. He and I discussed it Thursday afternoon.

"I figured we'd go out by ourselves tomorrow night," he said. "In fact, I'd planned for you and me to go back to the disco."

"We can go to the disco Saturday night if you

want, Derek." I put my fingertips on his cheek, tracing the outline of his jaw. "Please. Angie's parties are fun and this will give you the chance to see my friends, away from school."

When he began to gnaw his lower lip, I dropped my hand. It took so long for him to answer I decided he probably wasn't planning to give me a reply.

"Derek . . . ?"

"Okay," he said finally. "We can always leave the party early if it gets to be too much of a drag. What do I bring? Booze or beer or what?"

"It will be Cokes. Nothing alcoholic."

"You've got to be kidding! This is supposed to be a party, isn't it?"

"Her parents don't allow anything but soft drinks."

"Do we also play Pin The Tail on the Donkey?"

I let his sarcasm pass.

"You won't need to bring anything — except me," I said brightly, making myself smile. He had no way of knowing how nervous the conversation made me feel.

Derek looked as bleak as if he'd just agreed to eat a ground glass sandwich. "If this shindig means that much to you, we'll give it a try, I guess," he went on in a tight voice. "But you'll owe me, Wendy. It seems to me we're deliberately planning to waste an evening, and that's stupid when you can date only on weekends."

"You'll enjoy yourself," I insisted, not at all sure he would.

The frightening thought nagged me that if Angie's party bored Derek, it might be the only one he would agree to go to. As much as I enjoyed being wtih him and feeling his arms around me, I didn't want to have to give up my longtime friends.

chapter
18

Friday night was one of the worst times of my life. Angie wasn't to blame because the party was fine — at least it was for everyone else. Derek not only ruined the evening for me, but he embarrassed me in front of my friends.

The trouble between us began when he picked me up at my house. As I got into his car I saw a fifth of whiskey on the front seat, the neck of the bottle protruding from a brown paper bag.

"Derek, you can't take that to Angie's!" I gasped. "I told you her parents won't permit it!"

"Who'll tell them? I'll bet the other fellows bring bottles."

"They won't."

"Aw, wise up, Wendy. A party calls for drinks. You're back in the Dark Ages again."

"If Mr. and Mrs. MacLawhorn see any liquor there, Angie won't be allowed to have any more parties. Everybody in our crowd knows it. I don't want to get her into trouble." I drew a deep breath.

"If you insist on that bottle, you can do it without me. I don't intend to go into Angie's unless you leave the whiskey in the car."

"Okay, okay," he growled. "I'll put it in the trunk. Satisfied now?"

I was tied in knots, but I tried to hide my feelings from him. Derek could turn on the charm when he wanted to, but that night wasn't one of those times. To my horror, he didn't put himself out to be pleasant to anyone, and as the night wore on he got into an argument with Wes over a tennis match that had been on TV. I had to choke back my emotions when I saw how condescending he acted toward my friends; once when Karen and I were sitting on the couch she whispered, "Is Derek always so sarcastic, Wendy?" I pretended not to hear her so I wouldn't have to answer. In fact, I don't think I spoke after that.

When the party finally broke up and we headed for the car, we saw Suzanne Howard and Todd Loring standing by Todd's car.

"Darn it all, I've got a flat and I don't have a spare," he moaned. "I'd better try to get us a ride tonight, and then I'll come back in the morning and change the tire."

"We'll take you," Derek said, then he put his arm around Suzanne's waist. "Right, Sue?" he smiled at her.

There was enough light from a street lamp for me to see Todd's angry expression and I wondered vaguely if my own face reflected my surprise. Derek seemed to be making a deliberate pass at Suzanne in front of her date and in front of me.

The four of us crowded into Derek's car with me

in the middle and Suzanne perched on Todd's lap.

"Derek, take me home first," I said, and the words were scarcely out of my mouth before he gave a speedy, "Okay. Will do."

Suzanne laughed and murmured, "Gosh, this is a dreamy car. I could ride in it forever."

"You name the time and place." Derek took his eyes off the road to gaze in her direction. "I'll show you what this engine can do."

We'd reached my house. I was too angry to do more than mutter a good night. Derek walked me part of the way to my front door and stood there until I was on the steps.

I wasn't merely hurt and angry; I was stunned. Derek, I decided as I hurried to my room and undressed, was trying to pay me back because I wouldn't let him take the whiskey into Angie's house. Or, maybe it was because he thought the party was dull; he wanted to make me uncomfortable since I'd insisted we go.

If that was the case, he had to be gloating. I'd never felt more uncomfortable at a party in my life.

Charlie hadn't been at Angie's. I hadn't asked if he'd been invited. I figured Angie deliberately left him out since it was such a small group it might be awkward with Charlie and me in the same room. As I got into bed I couldn't help wondering what Charlie's reaction to Derek would have been.

Turning over, I plumped my pillow hard and closed my eyes, but sleep was a long, long, time coming.

At breakfast the next morning, Saturday, Mom asked about the party and I gave a vague answer.

"It was okay," I murmured. "Nothing super, though."

"Wendy, is something wrong?"

I needed to sort out my personal thoughts before talking about them. "I'm not sure if something is wrong or not," I said slowly and picked up half a slice of toast, breaking it into tiny bits. "Derek didn't enjoy himself last night and he didn't try to hide the fact. I gave him credit for having more manners than that."

"Does it make a difference in the way you feel about him?"

"Yes," I admitted. "It does."

I decided not to leave the house in case Derek phoned. It was an endless morning, another iffy April day with showers one minute and sunshine the next. I attempted to study but gave up because concentrating was impossible; to keep busy, I vacuumed the upstairs for Mom. We had a sandwich lunch and, early in the afternoon, she and Dad went out to buy groceries.

There hadn't been a word from Derek. The waiting brought me to my senses, and I realized no boy was worth the kind of anger I was feeling. At least Charlie had been decent enough to tell me what was on his mind.

In the den I moved restlessly from the couch to a chair and back to the couch. At quarter to three when the phone finally sounded, I jumped. Derek's "Hi, Wendy" was as casual as if everything was fine between us.

"What time do you want to go to the disco tonight?" he asked.

I didn't waste time on niceties. "You and I need to talk and the sooner we do it, the better," I said. "And I want it to be in person, not over the phone."

His quick intake of breath came over the wire. "If you have something to say, Wendy, spill it out," he snapped.

"Not over the phone." I said firmly.

"What the hell are you trying to do?"

My parents might come home momentarily, and I didn't want my conversation with Derek to be interrupted which made my house a poor choice of places. Derek's car was also a no-no. Once I was in the car with him, his kisses could keep us from discussing what had to be discussed.

I looked at my watch. It was four minutes past three o'clock. My brain seemed to be operating at peak efficiency despite the quivery way I felt.

"Derek, there's a coffee shop called The Blue Cup at Wayfarers' Shopping Mall," I said. "I'll meet you there at three-thirty."

There was a pause before he grunted, "Okay," and hung up.

I'd never been inside The Blue Cup. It was a place older people frequented, not teenagers, and I'd chosen it deliberately because we wouldn't be likely to bump into our friends there. Wayfarers' Mall was only a few blocks from my house, a ten-minute walk at most, and if Derek and I were in a public place, we'd be more likely to keep our voices down. Maybe . . . just maybe . . . we wouldn't fight if we were in the coffee shop. I knew what I'd tell him: that I'd decided not to see him anymore, but I wanted us to part on friendly terms.

chapter
19

Hurriedly brushing my hair, I sprayed on cologne and stopped just long enough to scribble a note to Mom saying: "Am with Derek."

Outside, the air was damp. The last shower hadn't been over long, and the streets were wet, raindrops shimmering on the grass and shrubs. I tried not to think about Derek and what I'd say to him if he didn't have a satisfactory explanation; instead I made myself concentrate on my surroundings. Pale, feathery leaves bloomed green on tree branches, and there were tulips and jonquils making splashes of color in the yards I passed. Forsythia was in full bloom everywhere, the bushes with their long, graceful tendrils cascading like yellow fountains.

I didn't know if paying attention to the signs of spring had a soothing effect on me or not, but I wanted to be calm when Derek and I talked. It was twenty-eight minutes past three when I went into The Blue Cup, and Derek wasn't there. *Well, somebody has to be first,* I reminded myself.

The restaurant was attractive with blue walls decorated with antique china platters and hanging baskets of ivy. Tables and chairs had been put in the center and along both sides, low curved benches upholstered in blue leather formed semicircular nooks.

"We don't serve meals until five, but we have delicious pastries and sandwiches, and anything you'd like to drink," the hostess said as she led me to one of the blue leather benches.

I told her I was waiting for a friend and would order later. Only a handful of tables were filled. Two men in the nook next to me were drinking coffee and arguing about baseball players. A lady eating a chocolate eclair had a magazine propped against her water glass, and three white-haired women were being served tea.

Time inched by. I felt sure I'd been there an hour, but it was just quarter to four. Another ten minutes passed. When the waitress inquired a second time if she could take my order, I said I'd like a lemonade although I was too jittery to enjoy it.

At ten minutes after four — forty minutes past the time Derek was to have met me — I didn't know whether to stay a little longer and hope he'd arrive, or admit to myself that he was standing me up. I decided to give him the benefit of the doubt and wait a few more minutes. Besides, the rain was falling again. That offered me a valid reason to sit where I was.

"Hello, Wendy."

At the sound of my name I looked up to see Jeff

Bryant. He was carrying a tray of napkins, knives, forks, and spoons, and apparently he was setting tables, although I'd been too engrossed in my personal thoughts to notice. I knew him very casually at school.

"Hi, Jeff," I answered. "I didn't know you worked here."

It was just something friendly to say. I didn't know anything about Jeff except that he was tall and clean-looking, with reddish brown hair and hazel eyes, and that he never cut up in class. It dawned on me I hadn't had a conversation with him since Christmas night when he was looking over the fire damage at Mallory's while Mark and Alan and I were there.

He put the last napkins into place and looked at me again. "Are you waiting for anybody?" he asked.

There was no reason for me to flush, but I did. "Sort of . . . I guess," I answered.

Jeff picked up the empty tray and I had the feeling he thought I was telling him to leave me alone. "My . . . uh . . . friend was to have been here at three-thirty, and I'm still here," I said quickly. "Talk about killing an afternoon . . ."

"Is that friend a fellow or a girl, Wendy? If it's a girl, I could sit here and gab with you until she shows. But if it's a boy, he might not like my cutting in on his territory."

"It's a boy." I squared my shoulders and took a deep breath. "But I don't happen to be anybody's 'territory.' Would your boss mind if you sat here with me?"

"My boss is my dad. My family owns The Blue Cup."

He smiled and I did, too, my face so stiff I realized it had been hours since I'd smiled, not since Derek and I got into his car to go to Angie's on Friday night.

Jeff sat opposite me, and we talked about school at first. When I'd seen him at Roosevelt High he was always quiet and rather reserved, but I discovered he had a lot of personality and a great sense of humor. We went from school to TV and movies and, while I was still upset over Derek's failure to come to The Blue Cup, chatting with Jeff made me relax. I didn't feel as desolate and tense as I had earlier.

"Wendy, I've always wanted to know you better," he said. "I guess you have dates for weeks in advance, though."

He was about to ask me for a date if I gave him any encouragement! I couldn't believe it! *That'll show you, Derek Hollis!* I thought, and the crazy thing was that I liked the idea of knowing Jeff better. The answer I gave him wasn't to spite Derek.

"I'm not dated up for weeks in advance, Jeff."

"Then I can call you?"

"That sounds like fun."

"It's short notice for tonight, but if you don't have anything big lined up — "

He cut the sentence off abruptly. I followed the direction of his eyes and saw Charlie coming toward us, rain dripping from his jacket. Jeff popped up from the blue bench like a jack-in-the-box. I realized he thought Charlie was the date I'd been expecting all afternoon.

The boys nodded to one another, and Jeff disappeared through a door marked EMPLOYEES ONLY.

I got out a hello to Charlie, my voice tense and tight.

"What are you doing here, Wendy?" Charlie asked as if he had the right to know everywhere I went and everything I did.

Before Thanksgiving weekend I wouldn't have minded because we were going steady, but now I did. It gave me an eerie sensation to realize this was the first time Charlie and I'd talked in months except to mumble greetings when we passed at school.

I gestured to the lemonade glass. "I came in for something to drink and to get out of the rain. What about you?"

"On Saturdays I'm still working at Sherrill's Drug, and this afternoon the delivery man left a package in the store by mistake. It's insulin for Miss Alexander, the hostess here. She's a diabetic and one of our regular customers, and Mr. Sherrill wanted to be sure she received it. He told me to knock off half an hour early and bring it to her on my way home."

A trickle of rain water slid from Charlie's hair down his cheek and he wiped it off with the back of his hand. The silence between us was uncomfortable.

"I was waiting for the rain to stop," I said.

"I thought you probably were meeting somebody here, Wendy."

"I . . . Yes . . . I mean, no . . ."

It was a stupid reply, and I didn't actually owe Charlie any explanations. I didn't want to tell him about Derek. But I'd never been able to pretend with Charlie. He knew I was upset.

"If you need a ride," he said, "I'll be glad to give you one."

It was twenty minutes after five, and I had nothing to say to Derek — *if* he put in an appearance. But I knew now he wasn't coming, and maybe he'd never intended to show up.

Nodding to Charlie, I got to my feet. Jeff Bryant was at the rear of the restaurant and when I stood, Jeff glanced toward Charlie and me, immediately becoming very busy lining up silverware on a table.

"Wait a sec, Charlie," I said, and walked over to Jeff.

"I see your guy finally showed, Wendy." There was a trace of disappointment in his voice.

I'd had enough hurts of my own to hate seeing another person snubbed.

"Charlie isn't the one I was waiting for," I told him. "Charlie and I live on the same block and he offered me a ride home because of the weather. Thanks for the good conversation."

Jeff continued to straighten the already-straight eating utensils. His "Sure" was followed by a shrug and the flicker of a smile. I had no way of telling whether he believed me or not.

My heart jumped as I got into Charlie's ten-year-old car, and I tried not to think about all the previous times I'd sat beside him on the familiar seat. We were uncommonly silent. Maybe he had his memories, too.

I gazed at the windshield wipers swishing back and forth in a struggle to keep the glass clear of water, and all of the sudden everything caught up with me. A sob started in the bottom of my stomach and rose up, up, up into my throat. With a choked, involuntary groan, I pressed both hands hard against my mouth.

"Are you all right?" Charlie asked.

I nodded. Closing my eyes, I said over and over to myself, *Don't cry, don't break down.* After a few minutes the car stopped and I had to open my eyes. We were parked in front of Roosevelt High School.

"Charlie, why did you come here?" I managed.

"Because nobody else will be hanging around school late on a Saturday afternoon. Something must have happened today to make you this upset and I want to help, but I can't unless I know what's wrong. That means you'll have to tell me — unless you don't want me to know. If I go home with you or take you to my house so we can talk, our families will figure we're dating again and that would be awkward as hell."

I might have smiled if I hadn't been so full of hurt. Trust Charlie to cover all the bases.

"In The Blue Cup you looked like you'd lost your last friend," he went on. "What did you mean when I said I thought you were meeting someone, and first you answered yes, then changed it to no?" His voice hardened. "Was that someone Derek Hollis?"

"Why do you ask?" I was on the defensive.

"Everybody knows you've been dating him a lot recently. I happen to think you can do better. A lot better."

"You can't tell me which boys to date, Charlie!"

"I know I can't." He slid his hands around the steering wheel. It was a gesture I'd seen him make dozens of times when he was trying to decide how to express his thoughts.

152

"But I do care about you," he added. "And I don't want to watch a no-good creep like Derek ruin your reputation and maybe break your heart at the same time."

"You're a fine one to talk, Charlie Peterson! *You* broke my heart last November!"

His face turned scarlet. "I know I hurt you," he said softly. "But I still think it was right for us to date other people. I just wish we could be friends now, though. If . . . if you don't want that, I guess I can see your point of view, but it won't make me stop trying to keep you away from jerks like Derek. You probably think I don't like him because he's so great-looking — and does he ever know it — and because he drives that sports car and has money growing out of his ears. But it's more than that. A lot more. He's no good, Wendy. Take my word for it."

"What are you trying to say?"

Charlie straightened up, sitting very tall in the car. "Derek has done a lot of bragging in the locker room at school," he answered. "He claims every time he dates a girl she's a challenge to him, and he says he keeps a record of his conquests."

I opened my mouth and couldn't manage to utter one word. I remembered exactly how Derek looked when he said, "You're a challenge to me, Wendy," only I hadn't known what sort of challenge he meant. Did he merely want to add me to his record? Had I been another name on his list and nothing more? I'd stupidly believed that he cared about me.

"Wendy . . ." Charlie's voice was filled with torment. "Wendy, please say something! Say anything!"

I made myself face him. He appeared as miserable as I was, and it got to me that he was trying to help me just as he might help his sister if he had one. At the same moment, I knew another fact: I loved Charlie, but I wasn't *in love* with him any longer. I'd been living in a dream world since Thanksgiving weekend. What I'd missed most since then wasn't his kisses, but his friendship; I hadn't been aware of it because until he broke up with me, I'd never gone out with another boy. Back then, I had nothing with which to compare my feelings.

Dad's remarks about kissing a lot of dates came back. It was smart advice, and it was exactly what Charlie was suggesting when he announced that he thought we should stop going steady. I hadn't understood before, but now I did. Now I was more grown-up, more mature.

Sitting in Charlie's car in front of Roosevelt High, I tried to say all those things — the words coming out haltingly at first — and then I told him about my stormy relationship with Derek. I mentioned how flattered I was that such a handsome boy would want me, and then I told him about Derek's possessiveness, and how he didn't want anything to do with my family or my friends.

"I don't think Derek Hollis is worth your worrying about, Wendy," he commented. "Kids at school already see through him. His bragging turns everybody off, but he isn't fooling anyone but himself."

The rain stopped. Two little boys down the block ran out of a house and put toy boats into the gutter, dancing around excitedly as the stream of water carried the little boats toward the corner.

154

"Remember when we used to do that after a rain?" Charlie grinned.

"Do I ever!"

"Wendy, know what I've hated doing without these last several months? Being friends with you. I could always talk to you. Share things with you. Good things and bad, and you wouldn't laugh when I was serious. There's not another soul I can say that about."

"You could always pull my ponytail — when I had a ponytail."

"If I needed to do it to get your attention."

Our eyes met and we laughed. Suddenly Charlie put his arm around my shoulders and gave me a quick hug, a friendly hug, not a romantic one. It was wonderful to be at ease with him again.

"We'd better go," I said. "Mom will be irked if I'm late for dinner."

Glancing at his watch, Charlie started the car.

Charlie dropped me at my house and I waved as he drove away. He held his hand out of the car window, his thumb and forefinger forming a circle with the other three fingers slightly curved in the "okay" sign.

Mom was in the living room. "Was that Charlie?" she asked in a stunned tone. "It looked like his car."

"He gave me a ride home from the shopping center. Don't act so surprised. He and I aren't dating again. We're just friends. Very good friends."

"But I thought you were with Derek this afternoon."

"That's over." I exhaled slowly. "Derek was impossible last night, and he stood me up this afternoon when I was supposed to have met him at Wayfarers' Mall. It doesn't matter, though. Derek and I don't think alike on enough topics for being with him to be much fun."

"I hope you're not too sorry, Wendy. Because I'm not. There's something about Derek I don't like, and I can't put my finger on it. Oh, by the way, a boy called you about fifteen minutes ago. Jeff — and I didn't get his last name. I told him you'd probably be in soon and to try again around six. He said he would."

I realized I was smiling. At that instant, the phone rang and I hurried into the den to answer it. Jeff was on the line.

"Wendy, I missed out when I tried to reach you a little while ago," he said. "But I'm glad you're home now. About tonight . . . if you aren't busy . . ."

"I'd love to see you tonight, Jeff," I told him, and my smile grew broader.

Life was clearer now. I had survived breaking up with Charlie, survived the loneliness and pain. I had stood up to Derek's attempt to add me to his list of "conquests" and was able to see him for what he was. I knew I could stand on my own two feet. I didn't have to be in love or going steady with a boy to enjoy a good boy-girl relationship. As I eased the phone down I realized that looking forward to seeing Jeff was making me smile.